LVE HATES VIOLENCE 2

BUT RETALIATION IS A MUST

DE'WAYNE
MARIS

GOOD 2 GO PUBLISHING

LOVE HATES VIOLENCE 2

Written by DE'WAYNE MARIS

Cover Design: Davida Baldwin – Odd Ball Designs

Typesetter: Mychea

ISBN: 9781947340374

Copyright © 2019 Good2Go Publishing

Published 2019 by Good2Go Publishing

7311 W. Glass Lane • Laveen, AZ 85339

www.good2gopublishing.com

https://twitter.com/good2gobooks

G2G@good2gopublishing.com

www.facebook.com/good2gopublishing

www.instagram.com/good2gopublishing

ACKNOWLEDGMENTS

To Sa'niyah, a free and loving spirit. Remember to always do you and remain as sweet as you are. Papa loves you!

And here's another round. Shout outs to Ralph, Virg, Martha, Daddyo, and the rest of my family. I love y'all.

And T.G., what up, bro? Miss you. Hope all is well.

And as for Jamall and James Brown from Compton. Good lookin' out, fam, on ya encouragement. Stay free so Pops can see you shine.

And for y'all, my readers out there, hope you will enjoy. Good lookin'.

The first few nights were rough. The frail little kid was not used to sleeping on slabs of concrete in a 5 x 8 cell, with nothing more than a sink and toilet made of steel.

The unfamiliar sight of the stale snot, which stuck to the walls to accompany the graffiti, was something new to the fragile little kid as well. He could not tell if it was that which kept him up all night, or the strange voices he heard from down the hallway calling out to him.

"Hey, where you from, homeboy?" or "I'm gonna rape your new booty!"

Another person would call out: "Hey, skinny boy, what ya in for?"

All of the noise drove him crazy throughout the night. He tried blocking it out, but he was unable to because he did not have a pillow to cover his ears with. All he had was the state-issued blanket he used to cover up as much of his body as he could, because of the freezing cold.

The lights inside the cell stayed on all night and only dimmed at the day's end—at "lights out" time. He found this was a term he would get used to for the duration of his stay.

~ ~ ~

The following morning, the frail kid woke up to the sounds of a loud cracking noise as the steel door opened up for chow. He was half asleep throughout the night, and by the time he was able to get into a solid sleep, it was time to start the day again.

When he stepped into the hallway, he encountered unfamiliar faces that he was almost sure belonged to those who taunted him throughout the night as he attempted to sleep.

He put his back to the wall and closed his door, watching as everyone else did the same.

He kept his head down and his eyes open as everybody made a single-file line down the hallway and into the chow hall. There he would eat his first breakfast as a prisoner and mark his territory as the lions did in the jungle.

One by one, each delinquent received his tray of food and sat down at the table in the exact order in which they had arrived.

Signs on the walls read, "No talking in the chow hall." And all that was heard were the clicks and clacks from the metal trays as the sporks claimed the items that were on them.

Heads were down as mouths were being filled. Everyone abided to the rules. That is, until he heard one of the voices from the prior night just before lights out.

"Hey, lil' punk. Where you from?" the deep voice barreled down the back of his neck like the heat from the sun.

At the sound of his voice, the place drew quiet. The click-clacking ceased as everyone in the chow hall waited for what came next.

The frail little kid never gave it a second thought as he stood up to confront the stranger that stood behind him.

He was the biggest of all the other ward in the facility, with muscles bulging from his T-shirt that frightened all the others—all except one.

Before the strange voice could say another word, the weak kid hit him with a quick two-piece to the gut, forcing him to hunch over. He followed up with a right hook to the jaw that made the other ward's body flop to the ground.

The incident happened so fast that the staff never realized what had happened until they pulled the new kid from the other's motionless body while he continued to pound him with vicious blows.

He walked out of the chow hall in metal braces with his chin held high like a soldier as the others watched. Altercations were nothing new in this environment, but there was something about the way the new kid threw those punches that had spectators stuck on stupid. They knew that if they ever saw him again, they would want no dealings on that level.

He spent a few nights in the hole while doing push-ups and sparring with his shadow, keeping brushed up in case he had to put down another demo.

His understanding was now in total contrast to when he had first arrived. This environment was no different from the streets, he thought as he continued to throw right hooks at his shadow as he bobbed and weaved.

"I can do this all day!" he said to no one in particular.

~ ~ ~

During his two weeks in the hole, he put together a routine in order to get through the long strung-out days of nothingness.

In the mornings, he would eat his breakfast and then read a few hours from some of Good2Go-published novels that were given to him by the librarian.

When she first came around, she asked what type of reading material interested him. And when he could not answer, being that he was unfamiliar with the names of authors and titles, she handed him his first urban novel. He had been hooked ever since.

After a few hours of reading, he would start his workout regimen, wash up when he was finished, eat chow, and then prepare for the day's end. This was when it got all bad—at lights out. This was the time that he would use his imagination to get through the night by thinking about his plans for the future, once he returned to the free world. And it did not hurt, he thought, to think about the pretty little librarian.

~ ~ ~

The two weeks had gone by fast—not like how he had expected.

He noticed that he had put on a few pounds, not of body fat but more like muscle mass. It was enough to make his biceps poke out from the tiny T-shirt he wore.

He was feeling different now as he walked down the hallway to his new cell.

The other youngsters stared at him. They were awestruck by the tiny frame of the adolescent that took down Biggems, the ward's biggest bully, with a three-piece combo that one could only catch on pay-per-view if he were lucky.

Mouths continued to drop as he made his entrance and met every stare with a "you can get it next" look on his face that made heads drop to the floor.

Most went back to doing what they were doing, with a smack from the lips that made a flat tire sound, pretending that they were not worried. But it was all good to Exavier, now that he had the juice.

Once he got to his cell to put his personals away, he unrolled his mattress and lay on his back, while looking up at the ceiling.

He reached into his pocket and pulled out the one thing that mattered the most and pasted it onto the wall.

The wallet-sized photo of his lovely mother holding him in her arms as an infant brought tears to his eyes. It was the one thing she sent him while in the hole, with no letter enclosed. Just an envelope with her funny little writing addressed to her son, with the little picture inside.

Although the package was small, it was the content inside and outside that gave it a sense of humor.

Her drawings of "I love you" hearts and lip prints, which seemed to be just as big as the envelope, were attempts to make him laugh.

She was twenty-nine years of age. And although she did drugs and Johns, she was still just as beautiful as when his dad had first met her.

Everyone called her Baby D, because of her resemblance to the young rap star from the group J. J. Fad, who was discovered in 1989 by Eazy-E from N.W.A., back in the days when the young ladies wore bob cuts in their hair with bamboo earrings and biker shorts.

Her real name was Dena, and she was stupid fly in her time. All the drug dealers wanted her, and Crawdad was the main one. She was fifteen when they first met, with Crawdad being twelve years her senior.

He was the owner of Jumbo BBQ, a small business that he used as a front to smuggle drugs and guns. He showered her with everything, including jewelry, clothes, and money. Dena knew how much he adored her too. So she kept her game tight every time he came around.

She knew that the only thing he wanted was sex, and she charged him to the game every chance she got. Then she came up with an excuse for why she was unable to have sex when it was time to get busy.

That is, until one day he was ready, and he was not taking no for an answer. He threatened to cut her off if she refused to give in this time, which meant no more jewelry, clothes, or money, and no more flossing on her homegirls in the new Lexus coupe that he had just bought for her.

She knew that losing the car was out of the

question, so she figured she would go ahead and give him a taste for the first time, especially since it already had been a year since they first met.

But that was when Crawdad decided he was going to have her forever, by poking holes in his condom. And just like that, her high school career was through and her life was in shambles.

~ ~ ~

"Ya cryin', dawg?" the voice caught him off guard.

But this time it was a voice that he recognized.

As he wiped the tears from his face, he looked at the picture on the wall with the envelope still in his hand.

The voice followed his eyes, recognizing the

young lady who used to flirt with him whenever he came over to visit.

"Is that Dena? Man, she was bad!"

He went over to the wall and snatched the small photo from the toothpaste that held it up, and put it to his face to get a better look.

"Is that your little ass all bundled up like a ball of crack?" he joked. "Damn, you was a lil' baby."

When he was finished looking at the photo, he smiled at his friend while placing it back on the wall.

"I didn't know you was in this block. What's good wit' ya?" Exavier asked, rising up from the concrete slab to embrace his friend who towered over him by six inches.

They grabbed each other and locked arms like true brothers. And you could tell that there was a deep sign of endearment as they hugged.

"Yeah, I'm holdin' shit down in here, homeboy. Heard 'bout that two-piece ya gave Biggems a few weeks ago. Everybody was talkin' 'bout that. About time somebody took his ass down."

It was actually a three-piece, and little Exavier was surprised that his boy, Midge, would subtract one. Because it was he who taught Exavier how to swing his fist like that in the first place.

"Yeah, I had to, dawg! If I had let that one go, that clown would've kept coming back. Ya know how this goes," he said while sitting back down on his bed. "There's a few more cats I might have to holla at before it's all said and done with," he continued.

Midge walked over to the door, which was slightly open, and peeked his head into the hallway to make sure that the coast was clear. Once he got confirmation, he closed the door all the way and then made his way over to the bunk, where his friend now lay on his back with his hands locked behind his head while looking up at the ceiling.

"Bay Nut was here. 1989."

At least that's what the graffiti said just above him, mingled with a bunch of other dates and gang monikers.

Exavier was in deep contemplation. So deep that he never saw it coming when Midge produced the homemade blade from his pocket as he sat down beside him while cupping his mouth.

"Whaaa!"

"Shhh!" Midge gestured through closed lips as he continued. "Don't trip, lil' homie. It's gonna be quick," he said as he pushed the blade through his gut.

"Word is they got Jim Jim for a hot one (murder) on that strap ya got caught with."

He took the blade out and shoved it in once again.

Midge watched as little Exavier's eyes filled with tears mixed with terror as his mouth moved beneath his fingers. This time, Midge put his hand over his face, hitting Exavier with the blade a third time under his rib cage, just below the heart.

Little Exavier's body stopped moving.

"Ya should have kept ya mouth shut, homeboy!" he whispered into his ear.

When he finished, Midge ran to the door, cracked it opened, and then peeked out like before to make sure the coast was clear, before moving down the hallway and back inside his own cell.

Once inside, he flushed his weapon down the toilet, washed his hands, and made his way to the dayroom area where others consumed their time with board games and playing spades.

LOVE HATES VIOLENCE 2

BUT RETALIATION IS A MUST

CHAPTER ONE

Bang 1
All Man Now

As Heath walked through the front door with Jai trailing behind, he navigated with his hands to turn on the light switch. It was dark and quiet, and Heath knew what time it was.

Heath had been going through this ever since Exavier came home from jail to live with him and his new bride. Each time he would walk through the door, Exavier would be sitting in the dark—in complete silence—with no appliances on. It was just him in the pitch-black room.

Heath became worried about his nephew, and so did Jai. She fell in love with Exavier when she first saw him—as a brother, that is—realizing that he was much older now than

Heath had described. But that was because his memory of little Exavier only went as far as eight years old, due to Heath's ten years away at the time of his incarceration.

Despite Exavier's mental disorder caused by the dramatic experiences that he endured in the juvenile detention center, Jai saw standing before her a man of resilience that had seemingly been through so much more than any young man had to go through coming up in his life.

When she heard his story, just like all women do, she wanted to find a way to fix him. And now that they were living under the same roof, Jai made it her duty to do just that.

"You need to see a doctor," Heath yelled as he went to hit the lights.

"Heath, please!" Jai pleaded as she walked

over to sit down with Exavier on the sofa. "He's just thinking, that's all! Cut him some slack," she continued.

Heath walked over to open the blinds and the patio doors to let in the fresh ocean breeze, allowing the rays from the sun to illuminate the darkness.

Little Exavier did not open his eyes until the beam of light hit the flesh of his face, causing his forehead to wrinkle. When he opened his eyes, he was dubious to the two images before him and unaware that they had made it home.

The undistinguished look on his face as he turned to Jai, seemed to tell her that it did not matter anyway. And Jai hated when he did this, since she was the one who, for the last two years, took care of him since being home. Heath ran his new bail bondsman business that he had just acquired.

Jai thought that part of what little Exavier was going through was because of his uncle's absence when he first came home.

Iron'RE stuck around to help keep an eye on the boy while they were on their honeymoon. But the moment they returned, Heath went straight to work at his new business in order to help support his wife and Exavier, since he was no longer in the game.

So it was Jai who had been dealing with the late-night sweats caused by the dreams he was having, or just sitting in the dark. He often scared the daylights out of her when she made trips to the restroom or to the refrigerator for a late-night snack.

At times she would just sit with him, listening to him describe how beautiful his mother was.

He would sit there with his shirt off while exposing his well-defined pecs and twelve-pack, which showed the three puncture wounds along with the ten-inch scar where the doctor had to perform surgery in order to save his life.

Exavier experienced so many hardships while inside. He fought every day, even catching a few stickings (stabbing assaults) against other inmates because he had to survive.

He also told Jai about the episode he experienced with the female detention nurse who had taken advantage of his growing body as the years went by. It only took him two visits before catching on and learning the true defin-ition of a head doctor.

He had no idea that he was being molested at the time. He just knew that he enjoyed the fact that each time he got into an altercation, he had to see the nurse, and he knew she would then serve him.

Jai thought it was cute when she first heard about it. But she had to check him one night when he went to hug up against her with a woody. And after setting him straight, she witnessed the bond between them grow stronger. They had become play brother and sister, which is why she had his back every time Heath got in his head.

He never told Heath all that had happened to him inside. And although Heath had spent most of his own life incarcerated, his experience was in total contrast to that of his little nephew.

So when it came time to console him, Heath did not know how to respond, which caused a block between the two since Exavier had come home. But he appreciated Jai for being there to pick up his slack.

"Baby, I told you he's been through a lot!" Jai said. "Go in there and talk to him. He needs that man in his life, and you're it!"

Jai straddled her husband in her laced gown while gyrating her hips just above his pelvis. It was after midnight now, and Jai was ready for round two, when Heath decided to take her advice.

"Hold up! Where you think you're going?" she demanded.

"You told me to go talk to him."

"Um, hello! I'm not finished with lil' Rocket Man yet."

"Little! I heard that. Ya know Mr. Rocket Man got that ass hooked. And just for that, you gonna have to wait!" he playfully responded, throwing his wife to the side to retrieve his pajama bottoms.

When he got up from the bed, he almost had a second thought as he looked back at his wife, who was now spread eagle across the bed in her laced teddy with her legs wide open, exposing her jewels, pleading him not to go just yet. But Heath stuck to his guns, giving her a kiss on the forehead before leaving the room.

"I'll be back," he said.

She lay there looking at the ceiling as he walked out the door, wishing that she had kept her mouth shut.

~ ~ ~

When he walked into the guest room where Exavier slept, he sat for a moment to watch the now-grown young man who slept peacefully under the covers as they rose up and down from his heavy breathing.

He looked at peace. So much at peace, that Heath was about to turn around and go back to his wife, until he felt her hands around his waist. Her bare chest rested against his back while the warmth from her breath blew at his skin as she whispered into his ear.

"Spend all the time you need with him," she said.

"And if I'm still asleep when you come back, just wake me up, daddy."

She was talking to Mr. Rocket Man this time, while her hand gripped his manhood through the fabric of his silk pajamas.

Jai kissed him as she turned to leave, while Heath thought about what to say to his little nephew so early in the morning.

There were five more hours until the sun would rise, and Heath thought what he had to say could have waited until later. But his wife was adamant. She saw something earlier once they had come home to the darkness and knew that it had to be addressed, but it had to be addressed with love. And as Heath continued to look at Exavier's sleeping body, the thought of his sister came to mind and suddenly reminded him of the promise that was made.

"I got you, Sis!" he said with a whisper.

~ ~ ~

For the past two years, a lot had been going on. The marriage, honeymoon, his new business, and the continuous love-making to his new wife caused Heath to forget about the well-being of his nephew.

He was under the impression that putting a roof over his head and providing him with food and clothing was sufficient. But he overlooked the dramatic ordeal Exavier had gone through during his incarceration.

The lifestyle that his mother provided for him was no walk in the park either, given that his sister was a drug addict. He knew that she meant well, but living under the conditions she provided was not good for a child.

Heath walked through the doorway toward the television and turned it off after turning on the lamp that set on the desk next to Exavier's laptop.

The light illuminated half of the room, to which Heath was grateful since his nephew was turned onto his side, slightly covered by the thick quilt that exposed his right buttocks.

Heath walked over to cover him up, until his nephew's body shifted toward him with his eyes open.

"Whaa!"

"Chill out, Nephew! Just covering ya mess," he said, still reaching for the quilt. "Ya got your whole backside out."

"What time is it?" Exavier asked.

"It's still too early, brah. Just wanted to talk to you a minute."

Exavier rose from the bed while reaching for his jeans to put on, oblivious to the fact that his uncle was standing there.

He walked over to his laptop, popped it open, and then turned it on to check the time. He looked back at Heath while sitting down at the desk to put on his slippers.

"Man, it's one in the morning!" he complained. "This can't wait until the sun comes up?" he now said, looking around the bed for his shirt.

"Don't nothing come to a sleeper but a

dream, pimp juice. Here!"

Heath threw him the shirt he was looking for—a fitted LRG with the signature letters blasted across the front.

Exavier threw on his shirt while Heath headed out the door and down the stairs to the patio.

Heath opened the door to the cool breeze from the Pacific Ocean and stepped outside. He could smell the salt and feel the rush as the waves pounded the rocks from the shore. Exavier was at his side a few moments later.

"I remember when I first came to get you from that place," he began. "I told you that I was gonna look out for you. I promised ya mother that before she passed."

Heath looked over at his nephew, who was looking out over the dark sea with his hands bracing the railing of the balcony with a strong grip. Heath turned to face him.

"Look, man. Since you've been home, I haven't been holding up my end of the bargain. I mean, how I was raised, ya word was bond. And if you can't keep that, what's left?" Heath turned back toward the ocean and continued. "I know you been through some shit in there. I can look at your knuckles and see that."

Exavier smiled as Heath continued.

"That's no way to live for a kid. The justice system was always fucked up. Think they doin' society justice by taking the kids from the streets. But then they place y'all in an environment that's just as bad with no hope of rehabilitation."

Heath jumped over the rail of the patio and landed onto the sand.

"Come on, Nephew, let's take a walk," he said.

The beach was closed, but Heath did not care. He figured that this was his backyard, with as much money as he paid for it. Iron'RE dropped six figures on the beach palace. And since he took up residence, the people grew to love him. So he was straight, he thought. If one of his white neighbors were to wake up and see two black guys walking down the beach this early in the morning, they would see that it was him and think twice about calling the law.

As they made their way to the ocean, Heath stopped just above the receding water and walked along the wet sand while Exavier followed.

Heath found the sound of the waves crashing against the rocky shores to be therapeutic as he inhaled the familiar aroma of the beach water.

He looked up at the darkness that covered the ocean, and for one split second he thought about Monte. Heath turned to look at his nephew, who was now walking with his head down and his hands in his pockets. Heath hoped that the ocean would be therapeutic for him as well. But it seemed that he was wrong.

As they approached the pier, Heath picked a spot close to the water and found a bench to sit down. Although the ocean was turbulent, Heath's decision to stop there was a peaceful one, he thought as he looked once again at his nephew.

"You miss ya mother."

It was more like a statement than a question. And judging from the young man's demeanor,

Heath knew the answer to that question before their feet touched the sand.

Heath planned for them to be alone. And he was glad that no one else was out, because he wanted his nephew to get the frustration out of his system. He knew that it was eating him alive.

But what Heath did not know was that little Exavier was about to expose something to him that he had been keeping bundled up inside for the past two years.

Exavier jumped up from the bench where he sat with his hands balled into fists.

He looked at his uncle and wondered how much longer it was going to take for him to figure out what the problem was. Since he had been home, it seemed to him that his uncle had been running away from the issue.

Exavier was not trying to go back to jail, but

he figured that with the reputation his uncle carried, he would have received word from the streets in regards to who had killed his mother and would have already handled business.

He knew that his uncle was with the business. He heard so many stories about him from his mother. But as time went by with nothing happening, Exavier was beginning to think that his uncle was getting soft.

"I know who killed her," he yelled out to the darkness while pacing back and forth. "I know who killed you, Mom, and they're gon' pay!" he yelled again, breaking down into his uncle's arms.

Heath reached for his nephew and held him tight. He knew that his nephew was not equipped with the proper tools to control his emotions. He could only imagine how difficult it was for Exavier all those years, discovering that his mother was brutally murdered and he was not there to save her.

Heath continued to hold Exavier as he wept, rubbing his back to comfort him. He reassured him that everything would be okay. But was it?

Heath started to think as he looked out toward the dark sea. He wondered how his sister would feel if she found out that he knew who killed her and yet did nothing to avenge her death. Part of him began to think that this was what he was afraid of. Digging into his sister's death would mean he would have to hit the streets.

He realized that it had been a few years since her murder. But he was certain that if he was to hit a few corners, he would be led in the right direction. But that meant that Heath would have to get back into the life.

He never did things halfway. When Heath first started his business, he put all his time into it to help it grow. And he watched as it flourished in the course of a two-year span. He got lost in his business on purpose—to help forget the past. He felt that going into business for himself would somehow right his wrongs and possibly make way to a promising future for himself, his wife, and, of course, little Exavier.

He looked down at Exavier and said, "Nephew, hold ya head up."

Exavier stopped the sobbing. As he lifted his head, the look on his face was a distinguished one, and one that Heath had experienced many times before. Right at that moment, Heath knew that they shared the same blood.

"Now, what did you mean when you said that

you know who killed my sister?"

Exavier removed his shirt in slow motion, gradually pulling the fabric across his head to reveal the wounds on his chest that left scars, detailing the reasons for his mother's tragic death.

Heath had a look of shock once he saw the vicious scars that intersected across his chest. He was surprised that he had not seen them before.

"Who did this to you, Nephew?" he demanded. "What happened?"

Exavier walked over to the railings overlooking the pier and grabbed hold to one of the bars before speaking. He told his uncle about his run-in with the law and how they found a pistol in his possession that was later discovered to have been involved in a murder.

He was later questioned by a detective who said that they had already had knowledge of Jim Jim being the trigger man and then passing the gun off to him to get rid of the evidence, but that they would need it in writing.

"I held my water though, Unc! I didn't tell them bastards anything!" Exavier exclaimed as he continued. "Jim Jim taught me better than that. The streets taught me better than that! You don't rat on nobody, no matter the circumstances."

"Ya did good, Nephew!"

Exavier walked back over to where his uncle stood.

"Then why did he do this to me?" he yelled as he hit his chest with his fist on top of the scars. "Why did he have my mother killed?"

Heath looked at his nephew and imagined

the pain the young solider had to have endured all those years.

Once the tears started to flow again, Heath did not know whether to hug him or just let him stand there and let it all out. He decided on the latter.

"Tell me everything, brah. It's gonna be okay. Tell me everything, and don't leave nothing out!" he said to Exavier as he continued to sob before going into the details.

"Well!" Exavier began. "For the past few years, I been hitting the block incognito."

His movements were animated now. It was almost like he came alive once he saw that his uncle was ready to get cracking. Heath was surprised at the sudden switch. The kid knew how to turn the waterworks off fast and swing right into motion. He was something impressive,

Heath thought.

Exavier continued as they both huddled on the pier in the wee hours of the morning while the ocean waves banged against the floor beneath them, imitating the rage that was bottled inside. It was about time, Exavier thought to himself as he told Heath about the detective who was having relations with his mother while feeding her crystal meth.

"I found out that she started selling for him later on after their affair. He was stealing the drugs from the evidence room after raiding the assays. He had a smooth operation. Jim Jim, Midge, and all my homeboys were tied in."

"Who the hell is this Midge?" Heath questioned.

"Midge is the one who did this!" He slapped his chest with the palm of his hand, making a loud cracking noise.

Heath looked at his nephew with admiration this time. He realized that Exavier was no longer the eight-year-old momma's boy that everyone loved. He smiled inside as the boy continued.

"Midge was the one that came into my cell with a shank and caught me slippin'," he said. "He hit me three times right here!"

His hand was still on his chest.

"What he do that for?" Heath asked.

He was furious this time, but more at himself for not recognizing his nephew's damaged past sooner.

Exavier continued, "They thought I told on Jim Jim when I got cracked with that pistol. I didn't know it had a body on it."

"Where is Jim Jim at now?"

"They gave him a life sentence. The streets

say he's doin' it big up in Lompoc Federal Prison." Exavier paused for a moment before he continued, "And guess who's lookin' out for him, Unc?"

"Who?"

"That crooked-ass detective that my mom was screwing around with. His name is Janikaski. Detective Janikaski!"

~ ~ ~

Heath was taking this all in. He was amazed at how much information his little nephew was able to gather. But he was saddened knowing that he had gone through all of this alone. He was suddenly glad that he had taken his wife's advice, and silently asked his sister for her forgiveness for not keeping it one hundred.

"This Janikaski detective," Heath began, "did he have anything to do with ya mom's death?"

Exavier looked over toward the ocean and then up at the stars. The sky was oblivious to their reality. He then looked back at his uncle before he responded.

"The same cat that did this," he started as he softly patted his chest this time, "did that to my mother and left her for dead in a motel room. Midge was working for Jim Jim, and he's the one that sent Midge at me in the detention center. And now that I found out that he was working for this detective, he may have killed her 'cause she knew somethin' she wasn't supposed to know."

"How did you find all this shit out?"

Heath realized how much he had been underestimating his little nephew. He thought he was still that little eight-year-old kid that he left behind to do his ten-year bid. But, man, was he wrong! This little nigga knew all he needed to

27

know.

Exavier told him that he had gotten his information from the boxing gym. That was the spot where cats gossiped like at the neighborhood barbershop, and the place where he spent several hours a day to spar with some of the best.

~ ~ ~

The sun was beginning to rise as they spent the last hour out by the sea to male bond and strategize on how to get revenge for his sister. They then headed back to Heath's condo to rest. But as for Heath, he would wake Jai out of her sleep with Mr. Rocket Man.

CHAPTER TWO

Bang 2
Johnny Law

After waking Jai and putting her to bed again with his magic stick, Heath got up to shit, shave, and bathe. He made himself a nice shot of coffee before he headed out to his place of business. He told Exavier to sit tight and stick to his normal routine until he was able to put something together. He really wanted Exavier to stay out of the way. But from the look in his eyes, he knew that was not going to happen.

As Heath jumped into his BMW 750, he smashed down Ocean Boulevard. He thought about calling Iron'RE. He knew that when he did so, he would be at his side within hours with the kids to help avenge his sister's death.

Heath hit a few buttons on his dashboard and an animated voice came through the speakers: "Calling Iron'RE now, Mr. Heath."

Heath was amazed at this new technology and was feeling kind of fly that the automated device recognized game.

It was actually his first time using the feature since owning the vehicle. He also found that this was a feature he could use, too.

He smashed up the 710 Freeway and headed to his office as Iron'RE's line continued to ring. Heath was doing 70 MPH in a 65-MPH zone when he noticed a narc car coming up fast behind him. He put on his blinkers to switch lanes in order to let the cop go by. But he became annoyed when he saw that the car had switched lanes with him, while riding hard on his bumper.

"Your car has been forwarded to an automated voicemail 835."

Heath pushed a button to disconnect the call as he kept a trained eye on the car behind him and the other on the road. He wondered why the dude was riding his tail so hard, but he quickly figured it out when the cop blurped him with his patrol light.

Heath thought it was unusual to get pulled over by an unmarked unit this early in the morning on the 710, especially when he was abiding by all rules and guidelines of the Highway Patrol Handbook. He had complied with everything, considering he was now a tax-paying, law-abiding citizen.

Heath pulled over to the right shoulder, put his car in park, and waited for the officer. He reached into the glove compartment for his registration and insurance. He also thought it would not hurt to point out to the approaching officer the little adhesive sticker in the corner of his lower driver's side window. It was of a badge supporting the local authorities, since he was now the owner of a bail bondsman business. He did not give a shit about the police, but he kept the sticker posted in the windshield just to floss.

The officer approached his vehicle with trepidation. He had one hand resting on his gun holster that was exposed under his suit jacket, while his other hand held his radio. Apparently, he was running Heath's plates.

Heath watched from his rear-view mirror as the officer stepped closer.

He was dressed in a suit and tie, which Heath found unusual for a routine traffic stop.

The officer knocked on his window and

asked for his license and registration. Heath rolled down his window and obliged the officer at his request.

He asked the officer why he was pulled over, but the officer ignored him by responding to the radio that was still in his hand.

Heath grew agitated with the officer's behavior as his past experiences with the law seemed to be resurfacing again.

He grabbed his steering wheel with both hands and a tight grip, attempting to hold back the anger that was brewing inside. He wanted to jump out of his car and do to the officer what they had done to Rodney King back in the day. But he stuck to the script of being a law-abiding citizen, while biting his bottom lip until the officer was ready to reason. Besides, with all the deadly shootings involving black drivers recently, he thought it would behoove him just to play his part.

He waited until the officer was finished running his plates to check for any possible warrants and found that there were none. The officer then returned Heath's papers so he could get on with his day, with no questions asked. But the shit did not turn out that way.

"Please step out of the car, sir."

The officer was brutal with his handling of Heath's car door when he pulled it open and demanded that he step out. The traffic continued to wisp by with passengers rubber-necking to view a scene that would be left to their imagination as they passed by. Many felt sorry for the driver as they caught a glimpse of the deceivingly corrupt policeman standing over the black man in his fancy car.

"Excuse me, Officer, but what is this about?" Heath questioned while hesitating for just a second before complying with the officer's command.

Heath was decked out in some slacks, a dress shirt, and a tie, with his briefcase sitting on the passenger seat. He thought the officer would give him a pass once he saw how professionally dressed he was. But the officer was persistent.

"Listen, I'm not going to ask you again, nigga! Get out of the fucking car!"

"Easy, pimp juice. No need to turn red. I got this," Heath said to himself.

Heath was confused for a minute. But he refused to let the situation get out of hand, so he went along with the officer's game—for now. He stepped from the car and smoothed out his slacks with the palm of his hands as the officer looked at him with disgust.

Heath taunted the officer further as he bent down to brush a hand across his gators to make himself clean before fully rising from the vehicle while looking the officer directly in the face.

They stood at eye level and about an arm's length away from each other with a look as if they were ready for battle, until Heath looked away and stepped in front of the car as he was ordered.

He knew the routine all too well, and he figured he had nothing to worry about in the first place.

"What's this all about, Officer?" he tried again as the officer searched his vehicle.

"Shut the fuck up!" the officer yelled as he briefly stuck his head out to respond. "I ask the questions around here. And right now I want you to be the fuck quiet while I finish doing my job."

The police officer stuck his head back inside, but Heath could still hear him talking.

"You black bastards think that just because you have a fancy car and good job that you can just do what the fuck you want."

Heath saw his lips still moving, but he stopped listening when he heard black bastards and almost lost it.

"Who the hell ya think ya talking to?" Heath asked as he emerged from the hood of his car and confronted the officer, who was now exiting Heath's vehicle after completing his search.

The officer drew his weapon and backed away from the driver. Heath looked at the man with a smirk on his face. Refusing to become another victim of an officer-involved shooting, he put his hands in the air.

"Tread lightly, my boy! I got a lawyer on speed dial," Heath warned.

"I don't give a damn about any lawyers. You continue to interfere with my job, and you won't be able to make that call. It's called obstruction, ya hear!"

The officer kept his firearm aimed at Heath as he continued.

"You're a three-time felon. You like to rob banks, huh? You did ten years in Federal prison and have been off parole for three years now. It seems like you've been doing well for yourself, Mr. Heath. Got married to a beautiful young lady, and got a place on the beach in Belmont Shores. Wow, good taste!"

Heath was surprised as he heard the officer recite his whole life script. How was he able to retrieve such information, he wondered. And as he continued to ponder, the real question was, why?

Cars continued to fly by while blowing their horns at the officer, with cell phones hanging out of the windows to let the officer know that they were recording.

The officer holstered his gun as he approached Heath to get all up in his tall can (face). The officer's breath smelled just like the officer's that got in his face after he was shot and handcuffed to the hospital bed years before.

Heath was fed up. He thought about grabbing the officer by the neck and twisting it just to listen to the bones snap. He could have done it with a snap of his fingers, he knew. Or he could have broken the bridge of his nose with a hammer punch, just so he could watch him bleed all over his nice suit. But, no, he knew this would undermine all he had accomplished, so he allowed the police officer to invade his personal space with his hot breath while he listened to him.

"Oh, how's your little nephew doing? Heard that he almost didn't make it outta that detention center," the officer said as he leaned in closer. "Too bad what happened to his mom. Not a good place to be when you lose a loved one."

Heath's eyes darted up at the officer. He was now putting together the pieces. Why couldn't he put it together earlier? Narc car. Officer riding solo and pulling him over to search his car. And for what?

Heath observed the man's description, and then he reflected on a conversation he had earlier on the beach with his nephew. White detective. Crooked. Tall. Slim. And then he remembered: Janikaski.

Heath stepped back a few inches to give them space before he began to speak.

"Janikaski. We finally meet, huh?"

Detective Janikaski was not surprised that Heath knew who he was. Jim Jim informed the detective that he heard from the inside that Exavier was trying to put together the pieces by asking all types of questions each day he came to the boxing gym to train. He asked about the crooked detective and Jim Jim being the connection to his mother's death.

"So, you know who I am. Good!"

"Yeah, I know you," Heath said.

"I know you're that crooked bastard who had something to do with my sister being murdered. I know who you are."

41

Heath then walked over to the driver's side of his car while passing the detective to climb inside.

He knew that this meeting was over, and he realized that it was just a scare tactic the detective attempted to deploy in order to get Heath shaking in his boots. But that was not happening.

"But I don't think you know me," Janikaski continued.

Heath started up the engine. He knew the man had said all he had to say.

"I could be ya worst nightmare. I don't give a fuck 'bout you or that badge," Heath said. "And I can see that you don't either!" Heath put his car in drive and added, "Have a good day, Officer."

And like that, Heath drove off into traffic.

~ ~ ~

"You little piece of shit!" Detective Janikaski said as he pulled off into the same traffic Heath had just moments before.

Little was an understatement, and the detective realized this early on when he ordered Heath to step out of his car. The two stood neck and neck. Heath had him beat by at least two hundred pounds of pure muscle. Yet the detective's heart—to him—was beyond measure.

He stood up to some of the roughest cats in his time. And in just about every case, he came out on top with his boot on their neck and placing bogus cases on most of them.

But today, for reasons unknown to him at the moment, Detective Janikaski found himself pissed off after his little meeting with Heath—the brother of the woman with whom he fell head over heels in love. And the woman he regret-

tably had to kill because of her big mouth.

CHAPTER 3

Bang 3
A Polish Swag

He always knew from the moment they met that her loose lips would someday be the death of her, because she was loud and free when speaking her mind.

It was the summer of 2009 when he first laid eyes on the mixed-race beauty of Creole descent.

The detective was riding around in his police cruiser and just so happened to make a stop at Costco for lunch. He ordered a few slices of pizza and a large Coke, and then took a seat at one of the vacant tables facing the parking lot.

It was a nice day outside, and customers seemed to agree as they entered the double doors of the wholesale store with smiles and laughter. It was very serene, which was in total contrast to the earlier events of the detective's day.

The Compton sheriff put a hit out on his operation and ordered every trap house they had under surveillance within the last two weeks to be raided.

It was simple for the detective to acquire the intel, even though he worked for another division. So on the days and times the raids were to take place, Detective Janikaski was able to relay to Jim Jim—who ran the operation—to close up shop, gather up all the cash and drugs, and then meet him so he could secure all the incriminating evidence.

The detective drove around for hours hitting several spots in Compton before meeting up with Jim Jim to pick up what he had asked for, hoping that he was not followed.

Now that the coast was clear, the detective sat at Costco stuffing his face with pizza and Coke, with over $90,000 in cash and three bricks of crystal meth in the trunk of his squad car.

He figured it was now time for a little peace and quiet while he filled his stomach. But his pretty Creole beauty did not allow that to happen.

She sat alone about two tables over with her cell phone glued to her ear while smoking on a Newport cigarette.

The sign read No Smoking in the area, but she did not care.

She blew smoke after each pull before setting down the cigarette on a paper plate where her pizza used to be as she talked through her cell phone.

"Yeah, bitch. That nigga had the audacity to tell me that I was cut off. Can you believe that?"

Detective Janikaski thought she was beautiful, with her light-skinned complexion that blended in with the sun's rays. She wore a cross-color outfit, a trend from the late '80s through the early '90s, that graced her body well with her bamboo earrings that peeked from beneath her straight and shiny jet-black hair, which touched her backbone. And when she raised the cigarette to her lips, the detective could not help but notice the perfectly manicured nails that sparkled rainbow colors. He was in love.

The detective had seen many chicks like her in the drug game. They were usually drug dealers' girls, so he knew that it frustrated him at times during the raid of a dope dealer's house—his real home and not the trap house—to see a fine chick like her laid up with a low life doing who knows what.

Honestly, the detective was actually jealous that it was not him who was laid up with a dime piece. He showed his fears by taking it out on the drug dealer when he would put his boot to his neck in front of her in order to show her who was really boss. It was an old trick he learned from Willy Lynch letters.

But as the years went by, and as his position elevated, Detective Janikaski mastered the game of imitation as he observed the swagger of the same men that he assumed to despise. After spending hours upon hours with these drug dealers, because they were turning state evidence to become confidential informants

(CIs), he was able to learn the game viciously. So now when anyone heard the Polish bastard speak, they would think he was a white version of Tupac resurrected.

That was how he got her. Because in spite of his pale skin and blue eyes, this good suit-wearing, clean-shaven, smelling-good-of-cologne bastard with a badge set a tone when he opened his mouth.

He walked over to her table and sat down without her permission, and studied her while she continued to talk on her phone. She was very much aware of the intruder, but she paid him no mind until she grew irritated by the man's stares and glares. At that point, she decided to confront him.

"Hold on, girl. There's some weirdo that just sat at my table eye-fucking me for the last three minutes," she complained over the phone while looking at the stranger. "Excuse me, what's your problem?" she barked at the intruder, unaware that the man was a detective.

He continued to look at her. But this time, a smile cracked in the corner of his mouth before he spoke.

"You too pretty to be letting such vain words come from lips like those," he said.

"Who the hell are you? Get the fuck away from my table with all that noise!"

The detective reached inside his suit jacket to produce his badge, before setting it down on the table. Her eyes opened wide once she saw the badge, and she cupped her mouth with her hand in surprise.

"Listen!" the detective began while leaning back in his chair to cross one leg over the other while smoothing out his tie. "Why do you have to be so loud and obnoxious, sweetheart? It's a beautiful day outside. People came here with their families to get a little peace and tranquility on this nice sunny day." He looked around as he continued, "The kids are enjoying themselves eating pizza and drinking Coke and cocoa. And here you are cussing up a storm while smoking these cancer sticks in a no-fly zone."

The detective leaned in to grab the cigarette from her lips, and put it out on her paper plate.

"Now what could possibly be wrong with something as perfect as you?" he questioned.

As he asked the question, she removed her hand from her mouth ready to speak.

"I'm so sorry, officer. I had no idea that you were a cop," she replied with a smile.

"I'm not. I'm a detective. Detective Janikaski," he said as he extended his hand as he spoke. "And you are?"

"Hi," she responded while smiling shyly. "My name is Dena. You not going to take me to jail, are you?"

"Well, that depends on something."

"On what?" she replied, aware that he was now flirting with her.

"On the likes of you giving me your number," he bargained.

And just like that, his world changed from being just a crooked detective to now being a crooked detective with the dope man's bitch. And, yes, he loved it.

~ ~ ~

After a quick reminiscence of his main squeeze who he had to kill, the detective regrouped so he was able to make some moves in order to put his plan in motion. But first he would have to pay a visit to Jim Jim at the Lompoc Federal Prison, so he could get the whole scoop on little Exavier and the boy's uncle, who he had to release. But only for the time being, he thought.

CHAPTER FOUR

Jim Jim sat inside his cell while he talked to his boy, Midge, on his cell phone to make sure that business was running smoothly on the streets.

He refused to let a life sentence stop him from shining. And as long as he had his top dawg checking his traps for him, he knew he was going to be all right.

Midge did what he was told and always complied to an order whenever it came time to execute. And that is what Jim Jim liked about the kid. He did not have to say things twice. He got it right on the first run, which is why Jim Jim had ordered him to kill his friend, Exavier, for allegedly ratting on him.

He later regretted his decision when the Feds came to visit him one day to inform him that someone in his camp was the one that snitched.

"But it was not the kid," he recalled the agent saying. "You just fucked up when you gave him the smoking gun that he ended up getting caught with, which made our case more solid. But he did not tell on you."

So now Jim Jim was sitting in the Federal prison for murdering a Federal agent, which was a favor for his detective friend. He was caught up because of his malpractice when he passed the murderous weapon to a youngster in his neighborhood instead of dismantling it, tossing it into the harbor, and charging it to the game.

"Make sure you pack that shit up right this time when you give it to my girl. The last one busted in ol' boy's stomach. It almost killed homeboy, ya dig?"

Jim Jim was referring to the heroin that Midge had bundled inside of balloons, so that his girl could easily smuggle the drugs into the prison. That is how Jim Jim ate; and although he had stacks of cash hidden in a safe place, he never stopped hustling. That is how he acquired his cell phone, canteen, and anything else he could get his hands on inside. He even paid the guards a few racks at a time so he could have conjugal visits with the various chicks that came to see him. Even they got a piece of the action.

He lay back on his bunk while continuing to talk to Midge on the phone.

"What's up with that lil' bastard asking questions 'bout his moms?" he demanded.

Midge told him about Exavier frequenting the

boxing gym to inquire about his mother's death and Midge's whereabouts.

"Oh, he wants to see you about that buck fifty you put in his chest, huh?" he said through the phone while he laughed. But then he got serious. "Well, you better be careful. I heard his uncle is back out, and I hear he's no joke."

"Jim Jim. Come on! Ya got a visit," the deep voice reverberated from outside of his cell as the door began to open.

The black guard stood at the doorway and waited while Jim Jim ended his call to put the phone back into its stash spot, a place that he knew not even the president himself could find.

"All right, soldier, I'll get back to you later. Candy's out there waiting on me," he said before hanging up.

He got up to remove the slab of concrete

from the floor that was perfectly cut, and placed his phone inside the makeshift compartment. The guard watched as he stashed his iPhone in the perfect hiding place with no worries. Because if this one had gotten confiscated, Jim Jim knew that he had five other cells that he could get to with phones inside.

Once he was finished, he put everything in order. He brushed himself off and then walked through the door of his cell and down the tier with the guard on his way to the visiting room.

"This bitch, Candy, is a straight freak!" he shared with the guard as they got onto the elevator.

He was smiling from ear and ear because he knew this was the week that he was supposed to take her down again.

But he became confused once he heard the

guard say, "This way. You have an attorney visit."

"On a weekend? I know who this is. Damn, this nigga is fuckin' my mojo up," he complained.

"It's that detective, that Polish thorn you got in ya side," the guard acknowledged. "You sure you can trust that dude?"

"That Polish thorn can be a cushion sometimes, Black. What ya in my business for anyway? Don't get shit twisted!" Jim Jim said while looking at the guard. "That Polish thorn be makin' it rain on the streets. Hell, you payin' ya mortgage off from that Polish thorn, so shut ya black ass up!" He looked at the guard before he continued. "Look, let's use this cracker for what they good for and get this money, okay?"

The guard opened the door to the attorney visiting room with a smirk on his face as he went back to his professionalism when he ordered Jim Jim to take a seat.

The guard and Jim Jim went way back to their days in middle school. They were both tighter than two babies in a crib. But one chose to make better decisions in life by turning to the Department of Corrections to become a Federal guard.

As Jim Jim took a seat, the guard left the room, closed the door behind him, and stood outside.

The room was small, but it was freshly painted a heavy gray, which gave it a gloomy tone.

Each time Jim Jim visited this room, he could only imagine how many tough cats he shared the environment with had come here to turn state evidence and just trade places with the one they were rolling over on. Pathetic, he thought as he looked around the room, before he finally reached out to greet the detective that sat across the table.

Detective Janikaski wore his full uniform, which was an expensive Armani suit. On the table was a folder filled with papers and his badge. He looked professional as if he were coming to question the very ones that Jim Jim despised in his mind just moments earlier. And that was what Detective Janikaski mastered. He was like a chameleon. He could switch it on and off so cold that not even his own kind recognized his deceit.

He kept a straight face until the guard had shut the door. He then waited a few seconds and scrambled through fake files before looking up to extend his hand and greet his associate.

From one's external vision, the detective and Jim Jim were like night and day. But deep down inside, the two of them shared the same ambition—and that was to boss up.

After the display of camaraderie, the two prepared to talk business. This time the detective took off his suit jacket to get comfort-table. He then sat back in his chair as if he was a real live hood nigga who was ready to have a meeting with one of his soldiers.

Surprisingly, he pulled out a couple of cigarettes and passed one to Jim Jim and lit up. The flame from his lighter continued to burn as Jim Jim leaned forward to get a light. After a few inhales and exhales, the detective spoke up first while the smoke climbed to the ceiling.

"I pulled over your boy, Heath, today," he said as he put his cigarette out on the table. "I was just temperature checking his ass to see where his head was at." He then leaned back into his chair as he continued. "And he's not an easy scare either!"

Jim Jim continued to pull on his cigarette, flicking the ashes onto the floor as he spoke.

"Why you sweatin', dude? I don't think he knows the scoop. He was up in here when all that shit with ya girl and her son went down." Jim Jim began as he got up from where he sat and walked over to the window. "Old boy ain't no joke. He got a cold rep in them streets. So you should be careful," he warned the detective.

"I'm always careful!"

Jim Jim looked at the detective when he spoke and thought about what Black said earlier while they were walking down the hallway.

"You sho you can trust that dude?"

The words echoed in his brain.

For a while now, Jim Jim thought about what the agents told him when he was first apprehended and convicted for the murder. He spent time on the down low, attempting to find out who the real snitch was. But so far he had come up empty-handed.

Initially, the detective that booked him had given him little to work with during the interview at the time of his capture, which is why he came to the conclusion that Exavier was the one that snitched when he got jacked up by law enforcement for the pistol. After having time to think about it, and sitting down with the cracker—with his fucked up grin on his face and the statement that he just made—Jim Jim thought that it was time that he started putting together all the pieces.

When he walked back over to sit down, he thumbed the cigarette out on the table, and dusted the butt and ashes onto the floor as if it was legal.

He followed the ashes as they fell to the floor. He then smiled when he thought about Candy and what he could be doing to her, had she come to visit him. She loved it when h-e would finger-bang her and then pull out the balloon after giving her an orgasm. He would then put his fingers in his mouth to taste her juices that covered it, before spitting the balloon back out and passing it to his crash dummy to smuggle back to the unit.

The operation ran smoothly, and Jim Jim wished that he could have been doing this instead of sitting in front of this clown, who he now began to realize he was doing this time for.

His smile faded as he looked up at the detective who was smoking on another cigarette with his legs crossed while blowing smoke up to the ceiling. They both sat there in silence before Jim Jim spoke again.

"Tell me," he began, "what you come here for today? Candy was supposed to come today and drop something off, but you're here. What's up?"

This time the detective put his cigarette out on the table. He pulled a handkerchief from his pocket to place the butt inside before speaking.

"I told Candy not to come today," he said as he got up from his chair.

He then walked around the table to the cigarette butt that Jim Jim had swatted to the floor and picked it up.

"I told her to get at you next week, and that you would understand. Call her when you get back to your cell."

He then put the handkerchief back into his pocket.

"What the fuck you do that for?" Jim Jim demanded as he slapped both hands onto the table while the two stared at each other before the detective spoke up.

"We have a problem. I came to tell you that we have to shut the operation down for a while."

"What you talkin' about, shut the operation down? We ain't shuttin' shit down!"

"Listen here, Jim Jim!" the detective shot back while sitting back down into his chair. "This is my operation, you hear me?" And if I say we shut shit down, then that's what we do!"

Detective Janikaski sat back and crossed his legs like before, with his shoulders leaned back and to the side as if he was a real nigga calling shots.

"Jim Jim, I'm the one who got you into this game," he reminded his partner.

"Yeah, you also got me in here for murder!"

"You got yourself in here for murder. That's what happens when you're careless," the detective replied while getting up to pace the floor. "I paid you real well for that. You should have gotten rid of the gun like I told you to, but I'm not here to talk about that. You made your bed; now it's time you lie in it."

Jim Jim studied the detective. His true colors were coming to life. He had been in the loop with Detective Janikaski for six years now, and he never imagined that their partnership would conclude like this.

Jim Jim sat in his chair, staring at the detective while he spoke. But he could not hear a word because he was listening to all the voices in his head that warned him early on in the game not to trust the white man. He put both of his hands on his head and then ran them all the way to the back of his neck in frustration before speaking.

"You know what, man? You got some nerve comin' in here like this. I'm doing life behind your bitch ass! And you gonna tell me some shit like that!"

The detective was laughing now. He saw no humor in himself being referred to as a female dog, but he actually did not mind that the remark came from him, considering the years that he had invested into their twisted partnership. But the irony was in the loyalty that Jim Jim showed to his bitch ass, he thought.

Jim Jim was sitting in there for murder that

he put him up to. He put a hit out on the little kid because he told him to. He sold all the dope he wanted to who, when, and where because he told him to. And he was the bitch!

"Look, we gotta shut shit down like I said. Trust me! It's either that or your whole team goes down and we won't have jack shit!"

"Well, what's going on, man? Ya still ain't tell' me nothing."

Jim Jim was cool now. Although he would no longer trust the detective, he decided to play it cool from there on out so he could get the full scoop.

"Why we have to shut it down?"

"They did a gang sweep all through the south LA streets, and two of our trap houses were hit. One was the safe house that was holding $500,000 in cash," he said.

Jim Jim listened as he spoke, while looking confused as to why Midge did not mention this over the phone. Televisions were prohibited, except in the dayroom, where he never went because his entertainment was on his cell phone 24/7.

"A few of ya boys took a fall," he continued. "And it's just a matter of time before they get to the other houses. So I'm calling it quits for the time being."

"Man, if you do that, then I'm just sittin' in this bitch for nothing!" he said.

Jim Jim was a real street nigga. Hustling ran through his veins, and he'd be damned if he was to let this clown stop him from eating.

"Can't we do something else like find another spot?" he asked. "Let's go take some shit up north and start some shit up that way. Midge could get a crew together and make it happen."

"Why are you so greedy? Don't you have enough money already?" Janikaski looked at his watch before continuing. "You should be up a few mil, ain't you?"

It was not a question. It was a matter of fact. Jim Jim was up even though he was sitting in a Federal prison with his life to give. But he had been a hustler all his life. So Janikaski telling him that it was over made him feel stillborn—dead to the world.

"Look, man, it ain't even about the money. This is my life we're talking about." Jim Jim stood up to pace the floor while the detective looked at his watch a second time. "If you pull the plug, it's almost like taking me off life support. I won't have nothin' to live for, dawg!"

This time the detective got up from his chair,

put on his suit jacket, and collected the papers in front of him. Little did Jim Jim know these were the words that the detective wanted to hear. There were no raids or gang sweeps. He just told him this to reinforce his story for why he was shutting down the operation.

Janikaski's objective was to get rid of Jim Jim because he knew that he had something on him. And that was the murder for hire on the Federal agent that Jim Jim got paid for doing.

The agent was undercover in the neighborhood while infiltrating someone well connected and in the game.

The law enforcement agency grew suspicious when it became rumored that Detective Janikaski was stealing loads of drugs from the evidence room and throwing them back onto the street to gross a net worth of $5 million each year. It was the job of the agent to entrap the detective in order to undermine his operation and bring down the detective and his crew.

His operation was in full effect, until one day the undercover agent caught the eye of Dena, the beautiful Creole gal with whom Detective Janikaski had fallen head over heels.

She fell in love with the black stallion, who reminded her of Idris Elba, the famous Brit actor that all the women loved. Each time he would come around to do business, Dena would go crazy with her blatant flirtatious behavior.

Janikaski's error was allowing Dena to tag along while he conducted business. They would meet at lavish restaurants or out at the pier on an expensive yacht. And each time, Dena would be there expressing the way her body was feeling with unspoken agreements.

After a few months, Dena told Janikaski she was leaving him and that he should be careful because the agent was on an undercover assignment to bring him down. Once he heard this, Janikaski put a plan in motion. He hired Jim Jim to knock the agent down.

It was more about jealousy than business, because when Dena heard what had happened to the agent, she went crazy. Janikaski could not see her having feelings like that for another man. In fear of her running her mouth to the local authorities, he had Jim Jim arrange for her death as well. Now all he had to do was eliminate his number one guy and he was all good, he thought to himself.

"Look, I came here today to tell you that I won't be supplying Midge and the others any longer," the detective began. "I say we lay low for a while until shit blows over, and then we'll take it from there."

Janikaski walked to the door and yelled for the guard to open it up. When Black did, Janikaski told Jim Jim that he would speak to him later and left him with the guard.

CHAPTER FIVE

Bang 5
Snake in the Grass

"I told you to be careful with that dude. I knew that he was lower than a snake in the grass," Black said as he walked Jim Jim back to his cell, while he strolled quietly listening to his childhood friend. "Word in the agency is they're about to send some agents ya way to question you about Agent Smiley's murder. They believe you didn't act alone, and that detective of yours was under some type of investigation."

Jim Jim waited until he made it to his cell before he responded.

"That bastard thinks I'm gonna take this shit lyin' down, then he got another thing comin'!" he said before going inside. "I been thinking about my situation over the past few years, and I'm starting to think that the little homie didn't have nothing to do with snitching on me. My eyes should've been wide open when those detectives got at me the first time." He then looked up at Black before he continued. "I ain't no snitch, so if them agents come knockin' at my door, I got nothin' for 'em," he replied.

"Even if they tell you that you could go home?"

"Look here, Black. They gonna have to bury me a 'G' before this nigga dishonors loyalty, even though I was betrayed by this punk-ass cracker! And if he did have something to do with me doing life, then we going to have to reach out and touch him," Jim Jim said before closing his cell door.

As he did so, he sat on his bunk and thought

about something the guard had said.

"Ya sure you could trust that dude?"

Black's words reverberated in his mind as the reality of them was seemingly coming to life.

Jim Jim removed a piece of plaster from under his bunk, dug out his cell phone, and made a call to Midge.

"We ain't shutting shit down!" he said to himself as his fingers scrolled to find the contact he was looking for. "And if I find out that it was you that got me clamped down, then it's on, cracker!" he said to himself again.

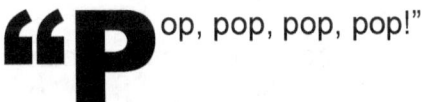op, pop, pop, pop!"

There was a split second behind each pop that all coordinated in a systematic rhythm. Exavier was behind the trigger squeezing with ease as each slug slammed into its target one by one, ripping to shreds the wax dummy he used for target practice.

The Desert Eagle barked with a majestic sound that made other shooters at the range jump with each squeeze as they watched first the head, then the arms, and finally the torso disappear.

Exavier was good with the tool, and Heath was surprised his nephew executed each shot with such poise.

The day was at ease, and the wind was just right as it carried the gun smoke upon its shoulders to a place in the atmosphere. Lil' Exavier was a beast each time he squeezed. He then looked up to the sky with a silent prayer to his mom to watch his back while he sought revenge.

"Nephew, where did you learn to shoot like that?" Heath asked as his cannon continued to bark like a vicious blue-nose pit bull.

In the absence of his childhood, Heath missed out on Exavier's upbringing on the streets of hard knocks. He was raised around some true monsters who recruited straight from the litter and bred boys into some real, live killers.

~ ~ ~

He recalled his first mission with Jim Jim. It was Midge and himself in the back seat of the car, with Jim Jim riding shotgun.

"I'm gonna show y'all how to put a real mission down," he told the two boys.

They both prepared for this moment at one of Jim Jim's undisclosed locations near the hills of the San Fernando Valley. There would be target practice with live rounds and combat training. Tonight was the night that it was going down, and Jim Jim wanted his two little protégés to tag along to witness the other side of his business—as a contract killer.

Jim Jim had been paid to knock down a key player in the game who was stepping on their toes when it came to business. He was a cat from the Bahamas that went by the name of Dante Majors. He had birds coming in from the tropical islands, like illegal immigrants across the Southern border, with AI Peruvian flake.

Majors sold each brick for a frugal price while killing the game in the southern central district. Detective Janikaski was not feeling that. He was good at shuffling the bricks around. But when it came to respecting the game, Majors could care less. His motto was to eat, eat, and eat more! And just like a fat pig that could not move because it ate too much, so was Majors when the black Impala pulled up on the side of his Bentley at a red light at 2:00 a.m. and blasted at the driver's side window before fleeing the scene.

The crime scene resembled the Tupac shooting in Vegas as multiple bullet holes tattooed the candy paint from the driver's side, leaving the passenger's side immaculate.

After the shooting, Jim Jim hit a few corners and torched the Impala before jumping into another car and driving off.

It was Exavier's first time witnessing a killing. And with the lifestyle he was now living, he was sure it would not be his last.

~ ~ ~

After hearing the story, Heath had to step back to take a good look at his nephew. He was sleeping on this young dude. The little man had been through a lot coming up, and he knew how the streets could be tough for any kid in the neighborhood. He wished that it did not have to be that way, he thought as he looked at his nephew, who was not little anymore with the Desert Eagle in his hand.

"That boy Jim Jim must be a beast," Heath said to Exavier while he reloaded.

Exavier loaded each bullet into the magazine with the expertise of a certified handler. And when he was finished, he slid the magazine in and pulled the cylinder back as one slid into the chamber. He looked up at his target and fired off three rounds before responding.

"I'm gonna kill that nigga when I get the chance!" he said, before he fired off the rest of the clip as all of the slugs went crashing into their target with a perfect hit. "Him and that bastard, Midge!" he continued as he turned to look at his uncle. "And whoever else had something to do with Mother's murder."

"Well, that chance may be soon enough," Heath said as he reached for his phone. It was the call he was waiting for. "And it looks like you're ready, too, nephew," he said as he answered.

~ ~ ~

Iron'RE was already in the city when Heath picked up.

He received a call from Jai, who was worried that Heath and his nephew were spending too much time at the shooting range. When she looked at Exavier now, he was no longer the sheltered kid that sat in the dark every time she came home. He was now wearing the look of someone on a mission. Exavier was hard set in finding the deception to shoot it right in the brain and kill the evil that sucked his mother into the game.

Jai never wanted her husband to get back in the life. He was doing so well. But she knew that Heath would pay homage to his sister by seeking revenge for her death. It was inevitable.

But she hoped that Iron'RE would be able to

talk some sense into him and get him to sweep it under the rug.

She felt bad for feeling selfish. But she did not want anything to get between the way she was living. Jai was living every woman's dream. She had it good while coming up, since her father took care of her from birth.

The Belgian Street thug had connections to a Canadian crime boss, and he showered her with all the material wealth that money could buy.

She was a boss at a young age. And everybody took a liking to her because she was not the type to floss her childhood privilege in the next bitch's face. Her mother was a beautiful Caucasian. Some would think that she would be at the bottom of the totem pole in an urban society when it came to popularity, but her light skin in the midst of the dark skin, low-income have-nots that gathered around her accepted Jai because she was seasoned.

Jai got all of her game from Kayla, who she met in high school when she was younger. Kayla watched one morning as Jai jumped out of the passenger seat of a maroon Maybach with her backpack strapped over her shoulder as she headed to the front door of the school. Her hair was brushed to the back and braided into a long ponytail that fell just above the back pockets of her jeans, which held on tight to her premature curves. She walked through the hallway to class as Kayla followed behind, absorbing the pleasant aroma of the mixed-race new booty.

Kayla made many attempts to get at her, but was respectively turned down by each one. But through all the rejection, there was something about Jai that Kayla was attracted to and that had something to do with more than just her sexual desire, which later brought them to become BFFs.

~ ~ ~

"What's up, bro?" Heath answered the phone after he removed his earplugs as he stepped a few feet away to remove himself from the sound of gunfire. "You down here in the city?" he asked while stepping even further away.

"What's going on, bro? Somebody shooting at you?" Iron'RE asked.

"Nah, me and Exavier are down here at the shooting range puttin' in a few shots," he replied, moving away even more. "When did you get into town?" he asked in surprise.

"Last night. Me and a few of the kids took a private jet to the Long Beach Airport. We're down at the safe house right now," he answered as he looked over at the kids who were posted in the den, unloading and cleaning the heavy artillery that was part of the cargo before he continued. "I brought a surprise for you, too."

"Surprise? What surprise?"

"Don't worry about it right now. I'll reveal it to you when we link up. How's later on tonight sound?" he inquired.

"You at the Baldwin Hills spot, right?"

"Affirmative," Iron'RE replied.

"I'll be over as soon as I pick up my wife from Kayla's spot and drop her off."

"Oh, speaking of your wife," Iron'RE remembered.

"What about her?"

"She called me a few days ago."

"Oh really. What did she say?"

"She was kind of worried about you and nephew. Said you were spending too much time at the shooting range," Iron'RE explained. "And she heard that little Exavier was looking into who killed his mother. She wanted me to talk to you about it. But you and I both know the only way I'm going to get in the middle of something is by your side. So whatever you need, brother, I got you."

Heath waited for a minute before answering as he looked toward the sky. He saw the smoke rising from the muzzles of cannons as they evicted deadly lead into their targets, and he smiled. He always knew that he could count on Iron'RE whenever he needed him for anything. And he was elated to know that it would be him by his side when everything went down.

He looked over at Exavier before respo-nding.

"We have an addition to the fam, bro," Heath told Iron'RE. "He's got my blood running all through his veins. Not scared of shit, and he's real good with the tool, too."

"That's good to know," Iron'RE said. "Bring him with you tonight."

"For sho! I already gave him the whole rundown on everything. But I need you to look into something for me, Iron'RE. This cop sweated me hard the other day. He knew my nickname and everything. My nephew said that he's more crooked than Rampart Division," he began as Iron'RE continued to listen. "This is the cat that was messing around with sis before she died. He was sweating me hard, like he was trying to rattle my chain or something."

"What you want me to do?" Iron'RE questioned.

"Get a locale for me. I wanna knock on this clown's door and let him know that he could be touched, too."

"No sweat! I know a young lady in the department who I can trust. See you tonight."

"Holla at ya then," Heath said before disconnecting the call.

~ ~ ~

Just like that, things were being set into motion, and there was no doubt in Heath's mind that a mini-war was likely to break out. From what he heard so far, he knew that the detective was in over his head. So in all aspects, he knew that the Polish menace was playing for keeps.

He looked over at Exavier and said a silent

prayer to his sis while alerting his nephew that it was time to go.

"**W**hat you doing? Oh, babes! What's all this?"

It was a lovely sight as they walked through the door. Rose petals welcomed her feet as she entered while taking off her stilettos and tossing them to the floor.

The aroma of oils fragranced the atmosphere as candles illuminated from the hallway to the bedroom. And before she knew it, Heath swept her off her feet while closing the door all in one motion and following the well-lit path to a lover's dynasty.

Heath laid her softly onto their bed next to a box of chocolate clusters and ripe strawberries. He then reached beneath her skirt to pull away her panties. His hand brushed against her vagina, picking up something wet and sticky along the way. He put a finger to his mouth to taste the juices that he collected as she watched and smiled.

"You like that?" she asked in a tantalizing voice.

Heath responded by pulling off his jeans and throwing them to the floor before climbing on top of her.

"Wait!" Jai hesitated. "What about Exavier?"

"He's not here right now, flower. I dropped him off at his chick's house. He'll be there until tomorrow. Right now, it's just me and you," he said as he began to kiss her mouth and then her ear.

Then he kissed her neck with the wetness of his tongue, sucking on her skin while she moaned. He made his way down to her torso, cupping her nipples with closed lips while running his tongue around the tips. She gasped as he bit one, provoking her pelvis to thrust into the base of his chest, where the tip of his phallus hung.

He put her legs onto his shoulder, allowing his tongue to taste the flesh of her inner thigh. He could smell the fruity flavor from the body wash she used hours ago. It made his dick jump moments later. He found his spot with his palate and took her into his mouth while his tongue played on her clit.

She screamed aloud, grabbing his head and pulling it forward while thrusting her pelvis even harder. Heath went to work on her for at least an hour with his head game.

~ ~ ~

"Whoa, boy, you ain't never slipped on your lovemaking! But tonight. Tonight was magnificent!" Jai exclaimed as she looked dead into his eyes.

"I love you, Heath," she proclaimed.

"I love you, too, flower."

~ ~ ~

As they lay together to watch a movie, he looked at his Rolex and realized that it was time to make a move.

He looked over at his wife, who was dozing in and out while her head nodded. He tapped her leg to wake her, and when she finally blinked her eyes, he told her that he had to make a run.

"Right now, baby? It's one in the morning!"

"I know, but Iron'RE is in town."

She looked at him with her eyes wide open this time.

"Yeah, he told me you called him."

"Baby, I wa—!"

"Shhh! I know." He put a finger to her lips. "I know you were just worried about me and Exavier." He let his hand drop to her thigh and caressed it. "But you know Iron'RE is a beast; and when you called and told him whatever you told him, he was already packed up and ready for battle."

Jai looked at him for a minute, and then she looked up at the ceiling as he continued.

"This cop pulled me over a few days ago. This crooked bastard!" he started to explain. "I told him that I was a licensed bail bondsman and ran my own business, but he wasn't trying to hear that," he said before he paused. "Well, Exavier found out that this was the same dude that my sister, Dena, was messing around with and possibly had something to do with her death."

Jai's mouth was wide open.

"He pulled me over for no reason and asked why Exavier was around the boxing gym asking about people—people in particular. And the story that my nephew's been giving is a big one, flower—a real big one!"

He jumped up from the bed to throw his jeans back on disregarding a quick shower, because he found himself pressed for time.

"I promised my sister that I would take care of him. And just a few days ago, I promised her again that I would avenge her death. Now ya know I make good on my promises, flower," he reminded her while buttoning up his jeans. "So don't worry about nothing, babes," he continued. "You know I will be safe."

Heath gave her no room to protest. When it came to business with Iron'RE, it was as if what she said did not matter anyway.

She sat there like a sad puppy, watching as Heath bounced back and forth to get ready.

He grabbed his pistol from the closet and stuck it in the holster that was under his shoulder. When he came back out, Jai was staring at him.

"That's why you was sucking on my pussy like that?" she asked. "So that I wouldn't put up no argument, huh?" Heath looked at her and smiled. "Come here, boy!"

As he lay across the bed, she softly grabbed his face with both hands and kissed his lips. "You come back safe, babes. You and Exavier, you hear me?"

"I hear you, flower, and I will. You gonna be

okay while I'm gone, huh?" he asked as he got up from the bed. "You know where everything is, right? Don't hesitate to call me if you need anything."

After kissing her on the lips, Heath was out the door.

When he left, Jai arose from the bed to check the locks to make sure the house was secured. She went back upstairs to their room and headed straight for the closet.

Designer clothes were hung up on hangers, some from the Wilshire District, while others were shipped in from overseas as far away as France and Italy.

Jai pushed the tasteful gear to the side to reveal what looked like a code box. When she pushed a few buttons, the back panel of the closest slid open to what appeared to be a warehouse of arsenals, which included semi-assault weapons like MAC-10s and MAC-11s with silencers that sat on red suede racks. The 9mms and a few Desert Eagles were pulled from drawers along with ample ammunition.

She did a survey on the heavy metal before closing the secret passage, pulling the hangers of clothes back to their location before exiting the closet.

When Jai went back to her bed, she lay under the covers and smelled the scent of her husband as her head rested on his pillow.

~ ~ ~

Heath was on the 710 Freeway in his Beemer approaching the connection to Interstate 405. Traffic was light, and Heath was glad it was in the wee hours of the morning, which meant that Johnny Law (the police) were off the beat and in the cut somewhere eating donuts. So his foot got heavy on the gas pedal with his phone in hand. His Bose speakers banged Kendrick Lamar's album *To Pimp a Butterfly*. He turned the music down when his phone rang.

"Iron'RE, what it do?"

The music faintly played in the background as Iron'RE spoke. He was in the office at Catch One night club when he made the call to Heath to inquire about his location.

The two agreed to meet at the safe house. But once the kids heard about the club and how it was cracking, Iron'RE thought that it would be good for them to let off some steam West Coast style.

Kayla ran the club now, which gave Jai a chance to look out for her new family and play her role as a good wife. Kayla was already there awaiting their arrival.

Since Jai and Heath had married, this was the first time Kayla saw Iron'RE. It was a shame what had happened to Que though; and for a long time, she wanted to ask about him but could not bring herself to do so.

As they walked inside, the kids stayed on the dance floor while Iron'RE went into the office to conduct business.

"Where you at, brother?" Iron'RE asked as he watched the computer.

"I'm just getting on the 405. I had to tighten things up at the crib so my wife wouldn't trip."

"Is everything okay with Jai?"

"Yeah, she straight, bro. I ran what she needed to know down to her, so she wouldn't worry, Plus, I had to spend some 'we' time," he said.

"I understand, brother," Iron'RE replied. "We're in here, so see you when you arrive."

"For sho!"

"Later."

~ ~ ~

When he pulled into the club's parking lot, the scene was no different from the two years since it had opened. This was where it all started, Heath thought. The life that he once knew had taken a major turn for the better.

When he stepped from his car, Heath surveyed the scenery. He wondered if the busybodies were aware of the murderous story that the parking lot concealed, like JoJo, Spider, and even Monte.

He wondered if JoJo or Spider was in some way reincarnated into one of the people in the parking lot, and he suddenly reached for his pistol before realizing that he was tripping.

"Man, let me get inside this club," he said to himself.

He walked around to the back alley by the bouncers as he greeted them by the front door.

As he passed the green bin where Monte's body was found, he did a Hail Mary salute, only because he knew that Monte was Catholic.

When he got to the door, he pressed a button. As a light from the camera flashed, he was buzzed in.

Two years had passed since the two had last seen each other. So their embrace was well overdue as the two big bodies—well over five hundred pounds when put together—smashed into each other while slapping and clasping with strong grips of endearment.

Iron'RE was ecstatic when he saw the kid. He was the one dude who he knew he could trust with his life if he had to.

Iron'RE walked over to the bar and offered Heath a drink. It was the same bar where his then future wife had pulled a gun on him. Heath smiled as he watched Iron'RE walk over to prepare the beverage and wondered if he saw any irony in his actions.

Iron'RE caught the expression.

"What's up, bro?" he inquired.

"Ya know that's the bar where my wife pulled that strap and almost got gangsta with you," he said with two fingers pointed in the air and his thumb up as if he was holding a pistol.

"Yes, it is," Iron'RE said with a smile. "But could you blame her?"

"I guess ya got a point. You are a beast, and

still buffin' that iron, huh?"

"Can't stop. You know it's a rush, brotha!" Iron'RE replied, referring to the steroids.

"When did ya start drinkin', brah? That's something new," Heath recognized Iron'RE was holding a bottle of Blue Dot Cîroc in his hand as he filled two shot glasses to the rim.

"It was on a jet with P. Diddy about a year ago on one of his extravaganzas to the Bahamas, and he broke out with one of these," he explained while holding up the bottle. "He tells me that it's one of his brands and that I should try it. Well, I just sold him a $2 million property up in the Hamptons, so he kind of peer-pressured me into taking a shot. And, brah, let me tell you, this is some good shit! Here!" Iron'RE said as he passed Heath the glass. Heath took it down with no hesitation and waited on his reaction.

"Real nice. Smooth!" he said.

After swallowing the liquid, Heath set down the shot glass while the foreign taste did its thing. Then he got onto a more serious note.

"Now that we are face-to-face, can I ask you a question?" he asked.

"Sure. What's up, bro?" Iron'RE replied.

He brought the bottle and his glass over to the futon and poured himself another shot, before setting the bottle on the floor to listen to his dawg.

"I heard about what supposedly happened to Que, and that he got into a terrible car accident that went up in flames."

Heath grabbed the bottle of Cîroc from the floor and poured himself another shot before continuing.

"I know that he got you for a whole lot of dough. And I know when that happens with anybody, there's no get-back from that."

Heath cut the last sentence short before putting the shot to his lips for another sip. His eyes stayed on Iron'RE as he did so.

"Say what it is that you want to say, my brother!" Iron'RE pushed with a smile, because he knew where Heath was heading.

Since the whole ordeal with Que, Heath began to feel some type of way since two years had passed being without his road dawg by his side. He felt kind of strange and thought Que had crossed the line, and he was hoping that Iron'RE had given him a pass. Although he told Jai he would for some strange reason, he was hoping that Iron'RE did not go back on his word. And not that he would, but Heath knew that betrayal was the one thing Iron'RE hated. So he had to ask.

"I'm going to just flat out ask," he began while looking Iron'RE dead in his eyes. "Did you smoke him?"

When Iron'RE got up to move to the computer, he was laughing. He motioned for Heath to join his side while he pushed a few buttons to the surveillance cameras as they captured the images.

The camera revealed two people from the parking lot emerging from a cherry-red Ferrari. When he zeroed in on the driver, Iron'RE pointed to the screen with his fingers. This was the surprise he was talking about.

This was how it was supposed to be two years ago, before things got ugly. And now Iron'RE wanted to make sure everything would go down the way it should, but there was only one glitch.

"This was the surprise I was telling you about over the phone," he reminded Heath.

"Who is that?"

Iron'RE pulled out his phone and dialed a number. He spoke for a few minutes and then placed the phone back into his pocket.

Iron'RE grabbed Heath by the arm and led him to the futon, where they sat moments before.

"You may want to sit down for this one," he said.

"Sit down for what?" Heath asked in confusion.

When the door to the office swung open, a man dressed in an expensive suit walked inside and closed the door behind him. Once inside, he made his way to the bar; and just as if he had been there before, he made himself a drink and took a seat behind the desk.

"Who is this?"

Heath was confused at the image before him. The stranger was nicely dressed in an Armani suit and sported gators on his feet and a $10,000 Rolex. He blended in well with the entourage, Heath thought to himself. But he didn't recognize his face.

The stranger got up to walk around the desk as he made his way over to Heath without saying a word.

The man smiled as he approached Heath. It was a gesture that caught Heath off guard, leaving him dubious as the stranger bent down within inches of his face.

Heath quickly jumped to his feet and literally

bumped shoulders with the stranger as he walked over to Iron'RE.

"Get the fuck outta here. No fuckin' way!"

Iron'RE stood at his side with a humongous grin on his face that said it all. The stranger came closer wearing the same grin.

"What's up, bro?" he said while reaching out to embrace the man he thought he would never see again.

"Que, is that really you, dawg?"

The two embraced while Heath reached for his face. He groped at his skin as if he was a father who had not seen his son in years.

Que's face had totally changed. The Belgian was no longer the same. Even the bones from his face had been restricted, giving him an appearance of a young Wesley Snipes. The plastic surgery was a hit. His identity was now changed from Quency Taylor to Goldie—Goldie Lane.

Although Heath knew that Que went against the grain, he was hoping that Iron'RE stuck to the script and did not allow his emotions to get the best of him. Que was family, and he felt somewhat guilty himself looking back at his actions when he committed to finding Que and attempted to bring him to his demise.

His wife made him feel it the most. Little Exavier was not the only issue that Heath was dealing with. He spent many late nights holding Jai in his arms as she sobbed for her father, who she just knew she would never see again. But now with the latest development, he knew Jai would be elated.

After the embrace, Heath stepped back to further examine Que and his newly acquired look. Heath had to admit that the boy was sharp. Que had not lost his touch when it came to checking out with the proper attire. The look fit him well.

"So, where does this put us?" Heath inquired. "Are you officially back with the family?"

Goldie walked over to his drink that was unattended and took a sip before responding.

"I hear you have a few issues that need to be addressed," he said as he poured himself another drink. "I made amends with Iron'RE, and we're straight," he said as he looked over at his friend. "And now I want to make right with you, bro. I'm all in, if you will allow me."

"Water under the bridge, fam. Come over here!" Que said as Heath reached out for another embrace. "We all good, fam. We all good!"

As they continued to chill in the back office, the kids were out on the floor trying to make it happen.

They partied on the regular back in Canada. But never was it cracking like the Catch, with real-live hood bitches camouflaged in their Versace and stilettos.

Then there were the studs that were dressed like them in loose slacks, button-down dress shirts, and a collection of gators that each kid wore.

The club was popping, and it was already in the wee hours of the morning when Dirt had three chicks surrounding him. They were dropping it to the floor as Snoop Dogg's "Drop It Like It's Hot" pounded through the speakers.

Dirt was one of the kids. Although he fell

short when it came to muscle mania like Iron'RE, Que, or Heath, he had the heart of a lion. He was also one of Iron'RE's secret weapons.

The six-foot-two kid with lengthy corn rolls was in rhythm with the beat, while all 170 pounds of him gyrated on the fluffy flesh. He had a live one, with two of her homegirls on either side of him doing their thing.

Some clowns on the sideline grew jealous of all the action he was getting as the other kids watched; and as they made their way over to Dirt to give him a heads-up, his phone vibrated in his pocket. When he went to grab it, he backed away from the fat derrière that bumped his pelvis, and slapped it before gathering the others to head to the back office. He never saw the haters, and it was a good thing that he had not.

He knew that it was Iron'RE when he looked at the text, which read "Game Time."

All seven soldiers sat in the small office plotting their next move. It was about to be like old times, with three main hitters back on deck. Iron'RE, Heath, and Que, whose name was now Goldie, were a force to be reckoned with. The other four young men that Iron'RE brought with him—Dirt, Rak, Cino, and Cap, which was short for Capone—were his up-and-coming protégés. So everything they did, or what they were about to do, was straight out of the book of Iron'RE's memoir.

"Where's your nephew?" Iron'RE asked Heath once they were all together.

"I dropped him off at his chick's crib. Don't trip. I can touch base with him when the sun comes up."

Iron'RE looked at Heath with affirmation as he continued on with the plot.

CHAPTER EIGHT

Bang 8
Game Time

"**Y**our honor, can we set a trial date for August 28, which would be, let me see," Ms. Gentry started, before she looked at her calendar while the judge waited patiently, "three weeks from today, your honor."

The judge agreed as did the district attorney, who sat under a pile of folders of overloaded cases that were sure to get an unfair representation.

"Thank you, your honor," the attorney replied.

She then got up to gather her cases and head up to the fifth floor to represent another client that was actually going to be sitting in the chair next to her.

The judge stared as she bent over to retrieve some papers that had fallen onto the floor. When she did so, her skirt rose up and exposed the thickness of her back thigh.

Ms. Gentry was thick and beautiful, and she resembled Nerissa Knight, the news anchor on *Crime Watch Daily*.

She knew that Judge Hitt was a freaky little bastard who always winked an eye or licked his lips at her whenever she came into his courtroom. She played on this each time to get her way within the means of rightful justice.

Ms. Gentry knew that the judge was expecting a reward for the extension she had asked for; and although the DA might have objected, she knew that the judge would overrule her. So she dropped the papers on purpose to give him a sneak peek.

"Trick bitch!" she said to herself through clenched teeth and a smile.

As she stood erect, she noticed her phone vibrating on the table. Ms. Gentry piled the papers neatly into her briefcase and closed it as she grabbed her phone and headed toward the hallway.

She placed her briefcase on the floor. It was 9:00 a.m., and she realized that she had at least thirty minutes to spare before seeing her first client.

The hallway was barely active. Only a few people stepped from the elevators in hopes that they were not late to see the judge for their infractions.

A Latino woman sat next to her with a crying baby as the mother tried to quiet her child with fries from a McDonald's bag, but the baby was not having it.

Ms. Gentry thought the baby was cute, with her curly baby hair and chubby cheeks. But the heavy wailing this early in the morning was annoying.

Ms. Gentry, who was now on the phone with an important call, suddenly looked over at the baby and understood why she never wanted kids.

"Hold on, Iron'RE," she said through the phone while grabbing her briefcase with an annoyed look on her face.

She turned to look at the Mexican lady with the crying baby before she walked over to the elevator and pressed a button. She looked back one last time at the helpless lady who could not seem to keep the baby quiet, and she felt sorry for her.

"Thank goodness for contraceptives," she whispered to herself before speaking through the phone again.

"Iron'RE, are you still there?" she asked while waiting for the elevator to open.

Iron'RE waited patiently on the other end, understanding that Ms. Gentry was at her profession, but hoping she had some progressive news for him.

"Shit, let me take the stairs," she said as she stomped away toward a door that read Stairwell, while dragging her briefcase.

"It's that bad, huh?" Iron'RE said.

"Nah, just this elevator is taking its sweet lil' time like I ain't got shit to do," she complained. "Then I got this Mexican lady with her crying lil' creature. Ohhh!" she complained again.

She pulled the door open once she made it

up the stairs to the fifth floor.

"I ain't lying, Iron'RE. I ain't never having kids," she said.

"Don't say that, baby girl. The world would be a better place if we had some little Barbara Gentrys running around."

"Boy, please! Ain't no room for one, two, or three of another me running around here. Do you know how bad that would be?" she joked.

This time, she was sitting on a bench alone in a quiet hallway of checkered marbled floors that led to several different courtrooms with the department numbers on the doors. Her client would be in department forty-three, and she was relieved when she saw that she sat in front of the right one.

"What can I do for you, Iron'RE?" she finally asked, on a serious note now. "I got a few minutes before I go in here to represent this clown for a bank robbery charge."

"Yeah?"

"Yeah," she replied. "And you want to hear something crazy? The dude went up in there with a brand-new BB gun that had the zip tie still tied onto the trigger and Vaseline on his face, thinking that it would blur his image from the cameras," she said while laughing over the phone. "And guess what his getaway vehicle was? Wait for it. A damn bicycle! Ha!"

Iron'RE laughed with her as she entertained him with the things she did for a living.

All bullshit aside, Ms. Gentry was a damn good attorney. And although she found her clients' situations amusing, she was certain that she would find a way to get the young black man a break.

"I got some news for you, by the way," she remembered now.

"The guy you asked about, the detective. He's a crooked son of a bitch. He's got so many complaints and investigations on him by the Internal Affairs Board (IAB), it's ridiculous. And you want to hear something else?"

"Give it to me."

"He's tied in with a bunch of crooked sheriffs in about three different departments."

"Oh really."

"Yeah, they call themselves the Screw-Face Boys. They're branded with a tattoo on their legs of a skeleton engulfed in flames and holding an assault rifle. They're very dangerous, Iron'RE. I got a homegirl of mine that dates one of them," she said.

"Where are some of the locations they hang

out? Do you know?"

"I can get that for you later. But I do know that they took over some bar in the Hollywood area. That's just one of their locations," she recollected.

"All right. Good looking out, sister. If you can, get a location on the detective guy, and where he lays his head so that I can pay him a visit."

"Sure thing, Iron'RE. I'll have that for you tonight," she said before the line grew quiet. She then thought before she continued. "How's Heath doing?"

The question surprised Iron'RE. A decade had passed since the two met in court, when Heath took the deal for ten years for the exact crime of the guy she was representing right now.

She must have been feeling guilty that she could not get him off, which was why she was asking about him in the first place, Iron'RE thought. But he saw there was no need for her concern.

"He's doing well, Barbara. He's flying straight now. No need to worry," he assured her.

"Oh, I'm not," she lied. "I just wanted to make sure that he's dealing with the outside okay."

"I know. I'll tell him you send yours," he responded. He waited for a minute before continuing. "I'll drop something into your account later on for your services, so be on the lookout."

"Okay, Iron'RE, thanks," she replied grace-fully. "They're calling me in for court. Call you later. Bye!"

~ ~ ~

Iron'RE hung up the phone and set it on the marbled counter in the kitchen.

They were back at the Baldwin Hills location where they spent the rest of the day plotting on how to take down Detective Janikaski and the rest of his crew. After speaking with Ms. Gentry, Iron'RE found out that their little operation was bigger than he had expected.

"We got a problem," Iron'RE said as he looked over at Heath.

Heath was at the dining room table playing with a MAC-11 that he had just pulled from the duffle bag. He grabbed a silencer and screwed it on to make sure it was a perfect fit.

While Iron'RE was on the phone, Heath was thinking about his wife. He told her that he would be gone for a week, because it would not be safe for him to return home until this was all over with.

He tried convincing her to spend a couple

nights at Kayla's to keep her company, but she refused and replied that she would be more comfortable in her own home with the familiar smell of her husband, even though he was not home.

This made him blush. He knew he had a real one the day they got married. And he knew that Jai was no punk and could handle her own if she needed to.

But the worry really came from how he was going to tell her that her father was back in town.

How would she react? Would she cry and go back into that depressed state that took him twelve long months to get her out of? Or would she take it with a grain of salt and keep it pushing?

After a long thought, he went with the latter, knowing that after spending two years with her—two good years—that she possessed all the qualities befitting a queen. And what queen did he know did not do well next to her king?

Heath looked up when he heard Iron'RE speak up.

"That was Barbara on the phone. This little mission, brotha, is much bigger than you think!"

He went into detail about how the detective was a major figure in the business, and also a major target for Internal Affairs and possibly the FBI.

"And get this," he continued, while walking around the marble counter. "She said that your boy was all in with a group of sheriffs that call themselves the Screw-Face Boys and are nothing nice."

Iron'RE sat down next to Heath.

"I know you're not worried about that though.

But it is imperative that we investigate at all levels before we get crackin'"

"Then what's our next move, Iron'RE?"

Heath sat there with a blue bandana in his hand, running it over the Uzi one last time to give it that spit shine. This was the tool he was going to use, Heath thought to himself, to bring the detective to his fate.

"Where's ya nephew?" Iron'RE asked before he looked down at the duffle bag and pulled out the rest of the guns. "He's our eyes and ears on this thing."

Exavier walked in with Dirt trailing behind him. His eyes lit up as he walked through the living room and into the dining room filled with all the artillery sprawled across the table. It looked like a gun bust had just gone down, Exavier thought. It was the kind that he saw on the news many times before when the ATF got involved.

Once he got over to the table, he greeted Heath with his special handshake before being introduced to the others as the kids emerged from the den.

"So this is the lil' man you've been telling me about, huh?"

As he stood up, Exavier realized that Iron'RE was a beast. His eyes grew amazingly large as he stood in front of the Hindu monster that was rarely seen to the world as anything different. The two bumped fists before Iron'RE sat back down into his chair to conduct business.

"Now that we're all here, it's time that I lay out a format to the measures that we must take in order to be successful in our mission." Iron'RE said before he looked over at the kids, who sat at the table. "This mission will be a little different. It involves certain members of law enforcement that have been tainted and therefore may be a little more than just dangerous."

Heath was dying inside with laughter as he heard him speak, but he kept a straight face. He did this each time he would give a speech. Iron'RE spoke with such eloquence, even when he was not trying.

At the embarkment of terrorizing some shit, Heath knew that all Iron'RE had to say was, "Nigga, let's go!" and they were there.

But Heath never intervened at all. He just sat there and let Iron'RE do his thing, because he knew that his friend knew what he was talking about.

"This is little Exavier," he said, pointing over toward the new recruit who was ready to put in some work. "He has a little more information that may shed some light."

Exavier took to the floor as he stood up from the table, and started pacing back and forth. His adrenalin started to pump, as he was full of excitement, while he slapped his fist hard against the palm of his hand as he went into detail.

He told them where to find Midge, the ring leader of the whole trap-house operation. He said that finding him would lead them to the main source.

Midge played hard, and he was tough, too, Exavier thought to himself. But looking at Iron'RE and his family of organized crime, he did not think Midge and his organization would stand a chance.

He knew that Midge was just a hood nigga

who did anything Jim Jim told him to do. Looking at the guns that sat on the table, Exavier knew Midge was not playing: AKs, SKs, semis, and automatics were next to bullet proof vests and grenades. They were ready for war.

~ ~ ~

The meeting lasted about twenty minutes before Iron'RE wrapped it up. They all agreed to meet up later to put everything in motion as Iron'RE told the kids to go out for the night and blow off a little steam.

Once the kids left the house, it was just Iron'RE, Heath, and Exavier. The two men talked over a couple of shots of Cîroc while Exavier listened on the sidelines.

When they found Midge, they would let Exavier handle his business for killing his mother; but afterward, he would get out of the way while the rest of them took care of business with the detective and his Screw-Face Boys syndicate.

When Exavier heard this, he stepped in.

"Hold up, Unc!" he interrupted as he slowly raised himself up from the table as he continued. "First and foremost, excuse me, Iron'RE, but I gotta say this."

Iron'RE looked in admiration as he watched the youngster stand his ground.

"Since I got out, you've been on my bumper as if I was still that lil' kid you left behind ten years ago."

"Ouch!" Heath thought to himself as his nephew continued.

His facial expression showed exactly what he was thinking as he took another sip from his glass and smiled.

"I ain't that kid no more!" he said. "And I thought we had this conversation at the shootin' range the other day. You sounded like you was feelin' me, and now you over here talkin' 'bout fouling me out after the first kill! That dude killed my momma! And you want to deprive me of my revenge? Nah, brah! I'm pushing with y'all on everything," Exavier announced out loud as he grabbed the Desert Eagle from the table and screwed on the silencer before sitting back down.

"And I ain't takin' no for an answer!" he said while grabbing his uncle's drink. He put it to his lips to finish the last of it before slamming the glass on the table. "Or I'll get my own revenge!" he warned.

When Iron'RE stood from the table, his chair almost crashed to the floor from the force of his legs as they aggressively erected.

Just as quickly as his presence grew across the table like the shadow of a grizzly bear, a burst of laugher erupted as he clapped his hands hard against each other in a trial of sequences while he jumped around in excitement.

"That's what I'm talking about, baby boy. Stand your ground!" he said as he looked over at Heath, who was feeling like Iron'RE was acting, but he kept it suppressed. "I think he's ready, Uncle Heath," Iron'RE said with amusement. "I can see it in the boy's eyes. What you think?"

Heath rose up from his seat and poured himself another shot from the Cîroc bottle. He knew that Iron'RE was feeling himself from the few shots he already had. But that wasn't enough to cloud his judgment, he thought. So as he finished the pour, Heath slowly raised the glass to his lips and said, "I got you, Nephew. I got you. That's exactly what I needed to hear. You in—all the way in!"

CHAPTER NINE

Bang 9
Blue Gossip

"**H**ey, call that nigga Turtle and ask him if he's done hookin' my foe up. It's been four months now, and that nigga should've been done. I shot his ass $10,000 a while ago," Jim Jim said while sitting on the stainless-steel toilet with his boxers down to his ankles while taking a dump. He had the curtain pulled in order to give himself privacy from his cellie as he sprayed a concoction made of Muslim oils and water that he used as an air freshener.

As he flushed, he told the caller to hold on. It was a long and powerful flush that seemed to have almost sucked in his testicles. He then continued his conversation after the flush.

"Yeah, on another note, I told you that his detective came through. He's talkin' about cuttin' the supply off and wants me to cut off the operation, but that nigga is smokin' if he thinks I'm gonna cut that umbilical cord," he said as Midge listened on the other end of line. "Said something about the Feds being on him or some shit, so he's scared."

Jim Jim got up from the toilet to pull up his boxers with the phone glued to his ear.

"Look here, Midge. After this next shipment is done, we not. The detective wants to cut it short, but I already got something in the mix," Jim Jim said as he went into detail. "There's this black and Asian cat in here called Asian Blac. He's gonna continue our load with a bunch of green (marijuana)," he said. "Dude is linked up with the Asian mafia up north in Sac. I'm in good with him too. Yeah, hooked him up with Candy, and she gave him a piece of that ass. And now the nigga is sprung."

"So, what you want me to do?"

This was the first time Midge had spoken on the phone with Jim Jim. He was lying back on the sofa while watching *Menace to Society* as he smoked on a blunt and listened.

"I gave him your contact. He's gonna call you at 3:00 in the morning, right after the guard does his last count. So be up!" Jim Jim informed as he started searching through his phone book as he continued. "You may have to take a trip up north to meet his people. Take Tracy with you, and you should be okay."

Once he found the number that he was looking for, he wrote it down and passed the paper to his cellie, who was on the top bunk on his own cell phone.

"Midge. We about to get into this weed dispensary business, my boy. The Asian got property down here, so we gonna link up and prosper where we can. Fuck that detective!" Jim Jim said.

Midge thought for a minute as the line went quiet.

"What's up, Jim Jim? You still there?" Midge asked.

"Yeah, yeah! I'm still here. Now listen. I think I messed up sending you at lil' Exavier like that—and his moms. I don't think that he had anything to do with me gettin' put in here. I think he kept it solid, dawg."

Jim Jim got up to walk to the cell door. He looked through the crack to make sure no guards were walking before continuing.

"Yeah, I'm almost sure that the detective snitched on me to cover his own ass. I got somebody lookin' into it right now, but I'll keep you posted," he said while sitting back onto his bunk. "But don't forget to be by ya phone tonight at 3:00 for Asian Blac. That's another mil ticket, my boy," he said before hanging up.

When he looked up at his bunkie, the other guy handed Jim Jim the phone he was on. Jim Jim spoke and then listened as the young lady's voice responded to his questions.

She was not aware at first of the name Jim Jim continued to mention, until she dug further into the matter and realized that the name mentioned was the exact name Iron'RE had inquired about.

Ms. Gentry knew Jim Jim from a few cases in the past. She represented him on a murder case, where he was acquitted because of her undeniable defense mechanism that put her in the league with the Johnnie Cochrans and other elite attorneys that were on top of their game.

The two had a love affair after the acquittal that lasted for three weeks before she called it off, because she was starting to fall in love with him.

Jim Jim had already fallen in lust with the mini-skirt-wearing beauty, who wore a different suit skirt each day during trial from designers such as Versace and Bottega Veneta. Each time she would reach for papers from the courtroom table, or walk up to the judge to hand him something, her skirt would press hard against her flesh to reveal her thickness.

Once the case was over, Jim Jim asked her out; and now, five years later, he and Ms. Gentry were still in contact.

"That's crazy!" Barbara said while going through her file where she found the name Janikaski and pulled out the information, which included a few photos and reports that she had acquired from an inside source.

The information was for Iron'RE, but once Jim Jim requested similar info, she made copies to mail to him as legal mail, so it would not be inspected by the CO without the inmate present.

"What's crazy?" he asked.

"Oh, it's nothing. I just have a client who's asking about this same dude."

"For real? Who is it?" Jim Jim asked as he slid to the edge of his bed with his ear pressed hard against the phone.

His cellie jumped down from his bunk and ran to the door because he thought he heard keys, but it was a false alarm.

"Who was askin' 'bout him, Barbara?"

Ms. Gentry hesitated to respond as she continued to look through the files, deciding on what to send Jim Jim that would not be considered incriminating.

"Sorry, Jim Jim, I can't divulge my client's identity, babes."

"You mean you won't!" he responded as he lay back on the bed with a smile.

He loved it when she talked like a lawyer, and she knew it, too, which is why she spoke in a mellow, dramatic tone.

"I can't, babes. If I do, I would be subjecting myself to possible disbarment if anything were to go wrong. I'm already breaching my position at the firm by talking to you on an illegal cell phone, which is contraband, might I add. Not to mention, you're incarcerated. How are you anyway? Have you been taking good care of yourself?"

She knew that the question would take the conversation into a different direction as Jim Jim started to paint a picture of how his daily routine consisted of perpetual redundancy, which forced him to continue in his criminality. He made her blush a few times while he recalled their three-week escapade that left her cum drunk and delirious. His tongue game was off the chain, he reminded her as he made smacking noises with his palate. This forced her to resist the temptation of pulling up her skirt and fingering the wetness that crept through her lips.

"Stop, Jim Jim! You know I'm at work!" she said.

"You in ya office, aren't you?"

The cell door opened for unlock as Jim Jim's cellmate walked out to the dayroom, closing the door behind him.

"I'm 'bout to hang up right now," he said.

"Why?"

"Because, my cellie just stepped out. I'm 'bout to shoot a video and send it to you, to remind you what you been missing."

"Ohhh!"

"Yeah, watch this. Be by ya phone in the next twenty minutes. I'm gonna have it greased up for you—all ten inches of it!" Jim Jim said before he hung up while Barbara sat back in her chair with a smile on her face.

It was not long before she let the thoughts of Jim Jim pass through her brain, before she sat up in her chair to get back to business. She went through the papers in front of her, but placed them back into the folder once she heard a knock at the door. As it opened, a well-dressed man stood in the doorway with some papers in his hand.

"You busy?" he asked.

"No, not really. What can I do for you, Montell?" she asked.

Just as she was speaking, her phone vibrated and an image appeared on its screen. "Ohh!"

"What's wrong?"

"Oh nothing," she lied as she nervously reached for the phone, flipping it over to its face. "Just a client, but what's up?"

"Oh nothing. I just wanted to come by to see if you were ready for your closing arguments tomorrow," he said.

"If you're speaking of the Williams case, I

sure am. Not too much to argue, the way the robbery was done," she said while reaching over to stamp some papers. "I mean, who robs a bank and uses a bicycle for a getaway vehicle?"

"Only the crazy ones, B!" he replied before he stepped inside her office all the way and handed her some papers. "Here you go."

"What's this?" she asked as she reached for the papers and leaned back in her chair as her lips moved silently reading the contents.

Montell then walked over to one of the chairs in front of her desk and took a seat.

The room was quiet for a long minute as she continued to read. Montell waited patiently as he watched her facial expressions change with each disturbing paragraph. When she got the photos, she was even more disgusted. She looked up at Montell.

"I know, but keep reading," he said.

There were more photos as her little fingers paged through them, stopping at one that made her gag. A young lady who was once beautiful now lay in the corner of a motel room. She was badly beaten with her throat slashed from ear to ear.

The one stiletto that was left on her foot, and her skirt that was raised above her waist to expose her goods, told a story of a promising night that went bad. In one of the photos, blood splatter was seen on the walls, which gave Ms. Gentry the impression that whoever this girl was, it looked like she put up a fight. The tip of her fingers and her knuckle were battered and bruised with blood stains that seemed already dried, which meant that her body had not been found for a couple of days, she thought. But she was not a pro at forensics.

The case was still open, and she saw that it had been for the past three years. When she looked at the report to find out who the investigating detective was, low and behold it was the infamous Detective Janikaski.

"This guy is just all over the place! What is he, some type of gangster?" she questioned.

"I hear he has connects."

"How did you get all this?"

"A female friend of mine works for the department. She was able to make a few moves for me."

Barbara closed the folder of papers and placed it on the desk. She wanted to pick up the phone to call Iron'RE, but she was afraid Jim Jim's testicles would pop up on the screen and she would blush. So she politely excused

Montell and thanked him for the favor.

"This is just between us, babes, okay?" she warned Montell.

Montell was a classmate, and they graduated together from law school. They both passed the bar and soon after developed a solid friendship, so she knew he could be trusted.

"I got you, Barb," he assured her.

~ ~ ~

"Today was a good day" is a famous bar from Ice Cube's *Good Day* rap song. He tells a story about everything going his way in a twenty-four-hour day in the streets in LA, while hitting corners in his rag-top Chevy on three-wheel motion with each turn dodging the haters, while not getting sweated by the LAPD.

"Today was going to be the same," Big Turtle said.

He wiped the remainder of the wax from the Dayton wires that were dipped in gold. The blue shell was flaked out in its wet paint while dropped to the ground, looking like a goddess getting pampered in a beauty salon.

Passersby honked their horns at the new creation as they drove by Orlie's Hydraulics, giving Turtle his props.

"This bitch gonna be killin' the show tonight!" he said, reaching into the window to grab the remote from the seat.

Barely touching the switch, the back bumper leveled out with the rest of the car and started to bounce on all four tires like an impala in the jungle.

"Just finished this shit early this morning," he said. "Yeah, spent the whole night giving it her final touch."

Midge was sitting in his Range Rover with the window down watching the power from the hydraulic pumps go to work.

"Oh, hit that shit, my nig! That shit is hot!"

When Midge jumped out of his car, he walked over to get a closer look. He opened the door to the coke-white interior that was trimmed in blue piping, and climbed inside.

"This muthafucka is on fire! You outdid yourself on this one!" he said.

"Yeah, I put all my energy in this one. Did it for my boy, Chub. I miss that nigga, bro."

Midge rubbed his hand across the dashboard, tracing the leather with his fingers.

"Yeah, that was cold what happened to my boy. You find out who did it?" he asked.

"Nothing yet, but I got my ears to the streets, and ya know how that bitch be runnin' her mouth. Something's gonna pop up. I gotta just have patience," Turtle exclaimed.

"Well, Jim Jim wanted me to come check up on this. We good?"

"Yeah, for sho! This baby is ready for the shaw. You seen I was just finger-banging them switches," Turtle said as he looked over at the garage. "Come in for a sec. Got some papers for you to sign."

"For sho, Big Turtle. Let me just tell ol' girl to wait for a minute."

"Bring her in with you. Who is that anyway?" Turtle inquired.

When she jumped out of the Rover, Big Turtle's head did a double-take. She walked toward him in her Gucci outfit and stilettos like she was on a runway, pulling off her glasses when she spoke.

"Hello!"

"What's up, momma? Right this way!"

Something looked familiar about this broad, but he could not put his finger on it. He escorted them to his office inside the garage as they took a seat.

Candy was mesmerized by the other low-riders that sat half exposed in car covers and the smell of the hydraulic oil that leaked from the pumps.

She used to low-ride years ago, but stopped when she got sick. Walking through the garage right now just brought back memories. She looked around to see all the model cars of the lowriders Turtle put together. As she continued to look, she saw photos of all those who put in work on the hopping legends, all huddled up in a group with smiles of satisfaction.

As she zoomed in on one of the photos, she immediately recognized Chub. But her heart never skipped a beat. She was no scared bitch, but she was cautious, which was why she excused herself. She told Midge that she had to make a call, and she would be waiting in the Range Rover until he was done.

"What's up with that broad?" Turtle asked as he watched her walk away. His antennae were still up since he first laid eyes on her. But he could not put a place to the face. "That's your girl, homie?" he asked.

"Nah, that's Candy. Some bitch that Jim Jim got running for him. She's thick as hell, huh?"

"Yeah, she is thick!" Turtle said under his breath.

But there was something about her that left the big homie mind-boggled. He knew that he had seen her somewhere before. Somewhere on Instagram, he thought to himself.

He let the thought dissipate because the contemplation was beginning to rack his brain. He then returned his focus to Jim Jim's lowrider.

"Aw, fuck it! Here you go!" he said, before he threw Midge the keys and had him sign a receipt. Although they were homies, he still kept the business separate. "He already paid me, so you all to the good. This bitch is ready for the shaw."

"Good looking out, Big Turtle. I'm gonna blast that nigga Jim Jim some pics of this bitch. Ya know he's gonna floss."

"Yeah, tell that nigga to let them know this is how Big Turtle gets down," he said.

"All the time, big homie!"

Big Turtle looked over at Midge for a

moment.

"Who's driving it back, you or old girl?" he questioned.

"I got that shit, my nig! She's gonna follow me in the Range."

~ ~ ~

When Midge emerged from the garage, Candy was already in the driver's seat of the Range Rover. She thought about making a call to Heath to let him know she was at Big Turtle's hydraulic shop, where she was looking at pictures of the owner and Chub embrace.

It had been two years since his tragic death, in which she had been an accomplice because of her tainted DNA that was running through his veins, before Heath delivered the fatal blow to the head with a shot from his Desert Eagle.

She never asked any question as to why

Chub, or any of the others she had infected, had it coming to them. She just knew that money talked and bullshit walked. Candy was like a black widow—the rare kind you would find in the ghetto. Just like in a spot where you least expected, she would bite you without you knowing it until it was too late. And she enjoyed it, along with all the expensive material that came with it.

She followed Midge as he pulled Blue Gossip, which is what they named the car, into traffic. The glass pipes made bubble noises as he smashed down Artesia Boulevard, hitting the switches as the sounds pumped through the speakers.

Midge rolled inside many lowriders before, but as he rolled in this one, he was feeling like the president. At every intersection, he stopped at the light like a superstar, making the ass drop and then rise up again when the light turned green.

Candy followed behind in the Range Rover as Midge clowned in the gutter lane, hitting the switches so hard that sparks flew from the metal frame beneath the bumper.

She pulled out her cell phone and made a call to Heath. When he picked up, she told him about the conversation she overheard between Midge and Big Turtle. She also mentioned that she saw a picture of Chub and Big Turtle embracing. They talked about a detective of whom she had no idea, and how Big Turtle was looking out for whoever was responsible for Chub's murder.

When Heath heard the news, he was glad that Candy had called him. She was a real soldier, he thought, and he was glad to have her on his team. But when he heard her say that she was with Midge, his antennae immediately went up.

"This Midge dude. Is this the cat that works for Jim Jim?" he asked.

Candy nodded through the phone as if Heath could read her mind, before saying, "Yes."

She told him that she and Jim Jim were messing around, and that she would love to discuss it with him later. She also told Heath that she would visit him almost every weekend and bring him work and have sex. So she saw Midge whenever she had to go see Jim Jim.

CHAPTER TEN

Bang 10
Dirt Nap

It was a year ago that little Exavier was at the peak of destruction. His days were short and his nights were long ones, because of his troubles with sleeping.

He stayed awake and alone in the dark, while the absence of his mother haunted him. When he was able to sleep, Exavier dreamt sweet dreams of her. He visited those moments of her warm embraces with hugs and kisses until the dreams would eventually turn into nightmares and he would wake up in a cold sweat.

Now little Exavier was on a mission. He was very much healthy and free from those nightmares as he made one last promise to avenge her death, and this time the demons believed him.

~ ~ ~

Exavier rolled down Central Avenue in the passenger seat, while Dirt drove the Range Rover, caressing the handle of the Desert Eagle that was stuffed inside his jeans.

They drove around armed as if it was legal, and it pretty much was for Dirt to do so. He had dual citizenship to the country, since he was originally from Canada. He was licensed to carry for employment reasons for a bogus bodyguard service for celebrities. If he ever were to get pulled over and checked by authorities, the search would come back legit, with proof that he worked with people like Justin Bieber, Selena Gomez, Britney Spears, and Nicki Minaj. So he was able to carry a pistol. As he drove, he was very much comfortable with the prospect of being pulled over.

On the other hand, Exavier knew the protocol when it came to being in possession of a firearm while being black in South Central Los Angeles. He warned Dirt that if the Feds got behind them, he was out of there. Exavier had a lot to learn about organized crime, Dirt thought, and he would be the one to teach him.

Dirt had him beat by several years when it came to age, but Exavier was like him in so many ways, Dirt thought, which drew the two together when they first met. As they got closer, Iron'RE saw fit that Dirt take him under his wing so that he could show him how the family business operated.

"Give me that pistol, my boy. I'll hold on to that until we reach our destination" Dirt said as he held out his hand as he drove, while Exavier reached into the waist of his jeans to grab the Desert Eagle. "Don't want you to become a track star if we get pulled over by Johnny Law?" he added while putting the gun in one of his empty holsters. "These thangs we try to avoid, young soldier, which is why everything has its place and order."

Dirt then reached into his glove compartment to produce a badge.

"You see his here? This is what I like to call immunity. If Johnny Law pulls us over, I tell him I'm armed and flash this little baby here, and we good."

He threw the wallet back into the compartment and closed it.

"I got this skeleton company in security," he explained. "Yeah, according to the job descripttion, we provide security to big-time celebrities, so it requires heavy armor. Cool, ain't it?"

"I feel ya, Dirt. But I don't know if you know about the officer-involved shootings that have been going on 'round here. They've been gunnin' us down with or without a tool. So if Johnny Law comes, I'm used to runnin'. I ain't trying to be next," Exavier warned.

"Yeah, I been hearin' about that all the way in Canada. Them dirtbags are scandalous for that. Canada is so calm. We ain't gotta worry about no shit like that!" he said as he entered the 110 Freeway and headed south.

"You pushing this Range Rover through the ghetto like this with a car full of guns got us stickin' out like a sore thumb," Exavier said as he looked out the window to see the Staples Center as they approached downtown. "Where we going anyway?"

Dirt got into the right lane and exited the freeway onto Fifth Street. He did not say anything for a minute. He just surveyed the streets as he drove, and looked side to side and then forward again as if he was lost.

He finally found the street he was looking for as he made a left on Broadway, and pulled into the parking stall of the city's large library. Dirt drove around and around the elevated ramp until he reached the top. He stopped near a Porsche 911 that was parked in the supervisor's space, near the parking spaces of other employees. He studied the license plate and almost laughed at the description. How ironic, he thought as he looked at his attire, which was a boss fit in his Tod's loafers. He knew who was boss, and it damn sure was not the unfortunate owner of the foreign vehicle he was now parked behind.

Dirt put the Range Rover in gear and started back down the ramp. Once he reached the bottom, he parked and sat for a minute to answer little Exavier's question.

"This Midge guy, how long you been knowing him?" he asked.

Exavier looked at him for a minute and started to wonder why Dirt was trying to change the conversation as they both sat in the Range Rover. Dirt reached over to the glove compartment and grabbed the badge that he showed Exavier earlier.

"That dude had something to do with ya mom being killed. I know that had to fuck you up bad," he said as he looked at Exavier and passed him the Desert Eagle. "Here, tuck this back into your jeans. You won't need it, but carry it just in case," he said while continuing to look at him. "You still haven't answered my question."

"I grew up with Midge," Exavier explained.

He pulled up his shirt to show Dirt what Midge had done to him while they were locked up.

"That ain't all he did. The bastard tried to kill me, but he didn't succeed."

He put his shirt back down while Dirt sat and listened.

"They thought I snitched on Jim Jim on a murder beef. But they were wrong. I held my water. But before I knew what was going on, it was too late. They took my mother's life."

Exavier then looked out the window. A couple walked hand in hand while he observed the cover of the book that he picked up at the library.

"What's up with this place?" he asked as he turned back to Dirt. "Why are we down here?"

"So much for the small talk," Dirt said as he looked at him. "Iron'RE wanted me to lace your boots up and show you how the family business works. To help avenge ya mother's death wasn't the only reason we came down here."

Dirt removed the pistol from the holster which sat under his armpit. He screwed on the silencer and continued.

"I'm a contract killer. I clean up shit for Iron'RE. It's a lucrative business. Nobody gets hurt but the ones the contract is on. And the kill is quick almost all the time, so they really don't feel a thing."

Dirt pulled the chamber back to see one in

the brain. He pulled the clip out to make sure that it was fully loaded, and then put it back in.

"This clown ran off with some of Iron'RE's merchandise, and now we're here to collect— his life, that is."

As Dirt jumped out of the Range Rover, he smoothed out his attire with his hand while looking into the reflection of the window to brush his wavy hair back into a ponytail. He looked like the average rich kid from Beverly Hills who may be attending a university somewhere and visiting the library for research.

No one would understand from where he received his nickname Dirt, until they saw how he really got down. Dirt was good with knives, explosives, and distributing poison to the right victim, not to mention, he was a well-trained marksman that worked well with any type of artillery that was placed in his hands.

As Exavier exited the SUV, he tugged at the waist of his jeans to hold up the pistol. From an amateur's point of view, he looked like he was ready. He was down for whatever. But when Dirt saw the expression on his face, he knew that Exavier did not know what he was getting himself into. But he did know that after today, Exavier would not have a problem with killing, after he saw how easy it was.

"On second thought, give me that, lil' brah. You good on this run," Dirt said as he gestured for the pistol in his waist as Exavier reluctantly handed it over. "This is gonna be an easy one," he admitted as he reached back inside to place the pistol into the glove compartment.

"Could you imagine that a supervisor for one of the major historical libraries in downtown LA is actually a wanna-be drug smuggler and dealer? The nerve!"

Dirt closed the door and walked to the back of the SUV to pop open the tailgate. When it came open, he grabbed a black briefcase and slammed it shut.

"This guy is smooth. Took us a minute to locate him," he said as he went on. "It's been about six months since he ran off with about fifty kilos of coke without payin'. He must have thought Iron'RE forgot, because he started slippin' on his routine, which led us to here."

Exavier listened while he talked. Dirt spoke real cool, but Exavier could tell that he meant business when it came to putting in some work. He had only witnessed an organized crime business on TV. He thought back for a minute as to how Jim Jim's business operated. They had Range Rovers and Benzes, too as well as big guns, money, and dope. And Jim Jim had hitters, too.

But for some reason, he got the sense that Jim Jim's clique, which he used to be a part of, was nowhere near as sophisticated and well managed as Iron'RE's clique. Of course, Jim Jim's clique was as gutter as any from some of the best books from G2Go Publishing—those urban books known for telling it like it is in the streets. Uncut. But Iron'RE's clique would be a best seller just as well.

Exavier was infatuated with just the presence of Iron'RE when they first met. His massive build and unfamiliar features of Indian descent were very uncommon to most eyes in South Central LA. When Exavier saw the long Mongolian running down the back of Iron'RE's expensive suit, he knew that he wanted one of those.

As they walked through the parking stall and out the front entrance, the sound of downtown's traffic boomed. Pedestrians crossed streets as the red lights halted cars to give them the right of way. The sounds of high heels and the beautiful smell of perfume lingered in the air as males and females passed each other without acknowledgment. They were all in a hurry to get to their destinations.

Skyscrapers touched the sky, while those inside watched the streets below and admired the daily activity from the spotless, mirror-tinted windows—compliments of the Clean Slate Window Cleaning Union.

Dirt walked with the briefcase in hand as they both arrived at the front entrance. Once they walked inside, they stood in line and waited to walk through the metal detector. Luckily, Dirt had placed his pistol and silencer into a secret compartment inside the briefcase that carried an undetected device to disarm the detector when he walked through. He knew that the detector would be there; and when they both looked at each other, he knew that he and Exavier were both thinking the same thing.

Once they made it through the metal detector, Dirt made a left into the lobby, which led to some elevators. Dirt looked on the wall next to the elevator buttons and saw a small directory and looked for the supervisor's name, floor, and office number.

The building was affixed with seventeen floors, three of which held huge shelves of books and computers that people could use for research. Floors five through ten were where people could go to observe different artifacts from history that dated back to medieval times.

Dirt ran his fingers across the directory past floors 11, 12, and 13—all the way to the word Supervisor and found the name, Glen Johnson, Head Supervisor of Christopher Columbus Library.

"Here we go," Dirt announced before he pushed the up button and they both stepped onto the elevator after the doors opened.

As they both stepped onto the empty elevator, Dirt pressed a button, and the elevator doors closed them inside. Dirt took a quick survey of the architectural mirrors which surrounded their presence, and he admired the sophisticated structure in which it was built. The sheer glass that traced the mirror's reflection made it look like a small piece of a medieval cathedral. And if you were the right person riding the elevator, you probably would have been amused by its theatrical flavor. The elevator music was not ordinary either. It sounded like it was from one of Shakespeare's plays, about whom Dirt was certain little Exavier knew nothing about when he looked over at him.

"You ever come to a library?" he asked as he looked up at the elevator's corner ceiling to see a little red light blinking. He already knew what Exavier's response was going to be when he saw the expression on his face. He pushed a second button, and the elevator stopped at floor 16.

When they exited the elevator, Exavier told him that the only time he ever experienced anything similar to a library was when he was in the hole at the juvenile detention center for putting hands on the biggest bull in there.

"Yeah, that was a dark place in my life at the time. But when the librarian came through with them urban books, I got my read on. And it didn't hurt to see her once a week either."

They both laughed when he said this. There was nothing on the planet better than seeing a beautiful woman every now and then while stuck in a dark place like prison.

When they got to the stairway, Dirt pushed open the door and they made their way up one flight of stairs to the 17th floor.

"I know what ya mean, dawg. I got locked up a few times when I was young, too," Dirt said as they continued up the stairs. "We had this nurse, man. She was so fine. I used to cut on myself just so I could see her to patch me up."

Exavier looked at Dirt as if he was crazy, but he understood him.

"You say you took down the bully of the joint, huh?" Dirt asked as he sized up Exavier and wondered if he was always this big.

"I ain't always been this big, dawg. I was a buck five when I first went inside. But I always had hands though," he said as he put his fists in the air like the boxers do in the ring.

"For sho! My boy. Say no mo'!"

Dirt knew that he would holla back at him later about that. He wanted to get the scoop on Exavier's fighting skills, because he liked fighting himself. But for now, he was getting ready for business as they approached the door to the 17th floor. There was something about those chameleon traits that each of Iron'RE's kids possessed, which made them one of a kind.

Exavier watched how smooth Dirt was as he placed the briefcase on the floor and popped it open. Dirt opened up the hidden compartment and pulled out the pistol as he continued to talk.

"I stopped the elevator on the 16th floor because I spotted a camera in the corner."

Exavier watched and listened as Dirt closed the briefcase and checked his pistol one last time.

"You could never be sure," he said as he pulled back the chamber again to make sure it was ready to go.

When he looked at his watch, he saw that it was 10:30 a.m., which was perfect because he knew from the few days he did surveillance that it was routine for Glen to be alone in his office around this time each day.

"There are no cameras on this floor, so be

cool, brah. We'll go to his office, walk right inside, and handle business. And we out, just like that. As smooth as a baby's ass. Ya got it, playboy?"

Dirt looked at Exavier's hands.

"Don't touch anything from here on out. Use ya fist when ya feel you gotta make contact with something. You don't want to leave prints."

Dirt had on a pair of thin leather gloves that blended in well with his attire.

As they got to the door, Dirt walked inside, and Exavier followed behind. Glen Johnson was sitting behind his desk with the phone to his ear as he spoke.

"Excuse me, how can—?"

Poof! Poof!

Dirt hit him with two rounds to the chest. Glen Johnson's body went back hard against the back of his chair before it came forward again.

Poof!

Another shot to the head as he lay there face down on the table.

Dirt walked over to his desk, grabbed the receiver, and put it to his ear. A male voice spoke softly through the other end as he said the dead man's name. Dirt hung up the phone and checked the man for a pulse. When he was sure he was dead, they both left quickly and quietly.

Text Good2Go at 31996 to receive new release updates via text message.

To order books, please fill out the order form below:
To order films please go to www.good2gofilms.com

Name: __ _____

Address:_____

City: _____ State: _____ Zip Code: _____

Phone:_____

Email:_____

Method of Payment: Check   VISA   MASTERCARD

Credit Card#:_ _____

Name as it appears on card: _____

Signature: _____

Item Name	Price	Qty	Amount
48 Hours to Die – Silk White	$14.99		
A Hustler's Dream - Ernest Morris	$14.99		
A Hustler's Dream 2 - Ernest Morris	$14.99		
A Thug's Devotion – J. L. Rose and J. M. McMillon	$14.99		
All Eyes on Tommy Gunz – Warren Holloway	$14.99		
Black Reign – Ernest Morris	$14.99		
Bloody Mayhem Down South – Trayvon Jackson	$14.99		
Bloody Mayhem Down South 2 – Trayvon Jackson	$14.99		
Business Is Business – Silk White	$14.99		
Business Is Business 2 – Silk White	$14.99		
Business Is Business 3 – Silk White	$14.99		
Cash In Cash Out – Assa Raymond Baker	$14.99		
Cash In Cash Out 2 - Assa Raymond Baker	$14.99		
Childhood Sweethearts – Jacob Spears	$14.99		
Childhood Sweethearts 2 – Jacob Spears	$14.99		
Childhood Sweethearts 3 - Jacob Spears	$14.99		
Childhood Sweethearts 4 - Jacob Spears	$14.99		
Connected To The Plug – Dwan Marquis Williams	$14.99		
Connected To The Plug 2 – Dwan Marquis Williams	$14.99		
Connected To The Plug 3 – Dwan Williams	$14.99		
Deadly Reunion – Ernest Morris	$14.99		
Dream's Life – Assa Raymond Baker	$14.99		
Flipping Numbers – Ernest Morris	$14.99		

Flipping Numbers 2 – Ernest Morris	$14.99		
He Loves Me, He Loves You Not - Mychea	$14.99		
He Loves Me, He Loves You Not 2 - Mychea	$14.99		
He Loves Me, He Loves You Not 3 - Mychea	$14.99		
He Loves Me, He Loves You Not 4 – Mychea	$14.99		
He Loves Me, He Loves You Not 5 – Mychea	$14.99		
Kings of the Block – Dwan Willams	$14.99		
Kings of the Block 2 – Dwan Willams	$14.99		
Lord of My Land – Jay Morrison	$14.99		
Lost and Turned Out – Ernest Morris	$14.99		
Love Hates Violence – De'Wayne Maris	$14.99		
Love Hates Violence 2 – De'Wayne Maris	$14.99		
Love Hates Violence 3 – De'Wayne Maris	$14.99		
Love Hates Violence 4 – De'Wayne Maris	$14.99		
Married To Da Streets – Silk White	$14.99		
M.E.R.C. - Make Every Rep Count Health and Fitness	$14.99		
Money Make Me Cum – Ernest Morris	$14.99		
My Besties – Asia Hill	$14.99		
My Besties 2 – Asia Hill	$14.99		
My Besties 3 – Asia Hill	$14.99		
My Besties 4 – Asia Hill	$14.99		
My Boyfriend's Wife - Mychea	$14.99		
My Boyfriend's Wife 2 – Mychea	$14.99		
My Brothers Envy – J. L. Rose	$14.99		
My Brothers Envy 2 – J. L. Rose	$14.99		
Naughty Housewives – Ernest Morris	$14.99		
Naughty Housewives 2 – Ernest Morris	$14.99		
Naughty Housewives 3 – Ernest Morris	$14.99		
Naughty Housewives 4 – Ernest Morris	$14.99		
Never Be The Same – Silk White	$14.99		
Shades of Revenge – Assa Raymond Baker	$14.99		

Slumped – Jason Brent	$14.99		
Someone's Gonna Get It – Mychea	$14.99		
Stranded – Silk White	$14.99		
Supreme & Justice – Ernest Morris	$14.99		
Supreme & Justice 2 – Ernest Morris	$14.99		
Supreme & Justice 3 – Ernest Morris	$14.99		
Tears of a Hustler - Silk White	$14.99		
Tears of a Hustler 2 - Silk White	$14.99		
Tears of a Hustler 3 - Silk White	$14.99		
Tears of a Hustler 4- Silk White	$14.99		
Tears of a Hustler 5 – Silk White	$14.99		
Tears of a Hustler 6 – Silk White	$14.99		
The Last Love Letter – Warren Holloway	$14.99		
The Last Love Letter 2 – Warren Holloway	$14.99		
The Panty Ripper - Reality Way	$14.99		
The Panty Ripper 3 – Reality Way	$14.99		
The Solution – Jay Morrison	$14.99		
The Teflon Queen – Silk White	$14.99		
The Teflon Queen 2 – Silk White	$14.99		
The Teflon Queen 3 – Silk White	$14.99		
The Teflon Queen 4 – Silk White	$14.99		
The Teflon Queen 5 – Silk White	$14.99		
The Teflon Queen 6 - Silk White	$14.99		
The Vacation – Silk White	$14.99		
Tied To A Boss - J.L. Rose	$14.99		
Tied To A Boss 2 - J.L. Rose	$14.99		
Tied To A Boss 3 - J.L. Rose	$14.99		
Tied To A Boss 4 - J.L. Rose	$14.99		
Tied To A Boss 5 - J.L. Rose	$14.99		
Time Is Money - Silk White	$14.99		
Tomorrow's Not Promised – Robert Torres	$14.99		
Tomorrow's Not Promised 2 – Robert Torres	$14.99		

Two Mask One Heart – Jacob Spears and Trayvon Jackson	$14.99		
Two Mask One Heart 2 – Jacob Spears and Trayvon Jackson	$14.99		
Two Mask One Heart 3 – Jacob Spears and Trayvon Jackson	$14.99		
Wrong Place Wrong Time – Silk White	$14.99		
Young Goonz – Reality Way	$14.99		
Subtotal:			
Tax:			
Shipping (Free) U.S. Media Mail:			
Total:			

Make Checks Payable To:
Good2Go Publishing
7311 W Glass Lane,
Laveen, AZ 85339